THE EX

WHO SAW A GHOST

Sally Berneathy

The Ex Who Saw a Ghost
Copyright ©2016 Sally Berneathy

Chapter One

Charley hovered next to Amanda at the table in the small Mexican restaurant in the Uptown area of Dallas, folded his arms, and scowled. "Four chairs? Just because I'm dead doesn't mean I'm not entitled to a place at the table. Since *that man* showed up, you don't treat me with any respect."

Amanda wanted to tell him he hadn't deserved any respect even before Jake came into her life, but she couldn't. The mere fact that her deceased ex-husband was tagging along on their double date with Teresa and Ross meant the evening had only a slim chance of success. If she began talking to a ghost, that slim chance would drop immediately to zero or lower.

Jake pulled out her chair and smiled, his dark eyes flashing with promises that could only happen if she got rid of Charley.

She returned the smile and sat. "Thank you."

He touched her shoulder and took a seat beside her.

"Teresa, I can't believe you're a part of this," Charley said.

Across the table Ross Minatelli settled Teresa Landow into her chair. She gave Charley a brief glance then returned to gazing deeply into Ross' eyes. It seemed to be their favorite activity.

Charley heaved a monumental ghostly sigh. "Traitors," he mumbled then went to sit at the bar.

A moment of relief, but it wouldn't last. When they were married and Charley was alive, he didn't spend a lot of time with her. Now that he was dead, she couldn't get rid of him. To be fair, it wasn't entirely his fault. An invisible tether kept him within a few hundred feet of her. Only Teresa with her psychic powers had been able to detach him for a few blissful hours. Teresa had promised to keep a rein on Charley if Amanda agreed to this double date, but so far she'd been less than helpful.

Their waiter, clad in an improbable matador costume, appeared to take drink orders.

"I'll have your Margarita Grande," Amanda said. "With salt." *And extra tequila. Lots of extra tequila.* Though there wasn't enough tequila in the world to banish Charley. She should probably focus on remaining sober so she could deal with Hurricane Charley.

"I'll have the same," Teresa said.

"Sounds good," Jake said, "since Ross is our designated driver."

"Iced tea for me. I don't need alcohol to get high. I just need this woman beside me." Ross grinned at Teresa.

She tilted her head to one side, looked at him and fluttered her long lashes. Her sleek, dark hair slid along her shoulders, and her lips slanted into a happy smile. Teresa was a different person from the stressed woman charged with her husband's murder that Amanda had met a month ago.

The waiter brought their drinks as well as a basket of chips and individual bowls of hot sauce.

Amanda sipped her drink, nibbled on chips, and studied the menu. Charley remained at the bar with his back turned to them. Maybe he'd stay there the rest of the evening.

Yeah, and maybe she'd win the lottery without buying a ticket. Same odds.

She reached for another chip at the same time as Jake. His hand touched hers and a tingle of electricity shot through her.

His expression told her the touch hadn't been an accident. Briefly he wrapped his fingers around hers then returned his gaze to the menu. "What looks good?" he asked.

You.

As if he could read her thoughts, Charley returned to their table. "It all looks good to a man who hasn't been able to eat or drink in..." His lips twisted into a strange expression. He was trying to lie. "In almost..." He grimaced and sighed. "In six months. That may not sound like a long time, but you people don't go more than a few hours without eating and drinking, and you don't even offer me anything anymore."

The last time Amanda and Teresa had come to this restaurant, they'd sat at a table outside, basking in the warm September evening. Teresa had made sure Charley had his own chair and had provided him with a margarita and a fajita which he'd claimed he could *almost taste*. She had talked to him and made him feel included...*almost alive*. Tonight they sat inside to avoid the chill of mid-October. The table's four chairs were all occupied so there was no room for Charley, and Teresa's attention was focused on Ross. Amanda could *almost* feel sorry for Charley. But not quite.

Teresa winked at Charley. "I recommend the fajitas. Amanda and I came here with a dear friend, and we all had the fajitas. It was a great evening."

Charley looked somewhat mollified at her reference to him as a dear friend and to their great evening.

Ross laid down his menu and took Teresa's hand. "I'll have the fajitas and anything else you think I should have."

Charley made a face. "What a stupid thing to say. Don't you think he sounds stupid, Teresa?"

Teresa's only response was a barely perceptible warning shake of her head.

Jake grinned. He was used to his buddy's instant and fleeting romances. "I'm good with fajitas. How about you, Amanda?"

Charley left Teresa's side and moved to the corner of the table between Jake and Amanda. "*How about you, Amanda*?" he mocked, leaning over to get in Jake's face. "Yeah, Daggett, she likes fajitas. Want to know how I know? I was married to her, that's how I know. I mean, I *am* married to her! And you have no right to be out here in public with *my wife*."

Amanda took another sip of her drink and gritted her teeth to keep from shouting at him. Charley had refused to sign the divorce papers in life. In his after life, he had a problem with the *till death do us part* element of the wedding vows.

She forced a smile. "Yes, Jake, fajitas sound great."

"*Yes, Jake, fajitas sound great.*" Charley punched Jake in the nose. His fist went through and came out the back of Jake's rumpled brown hair.

Jake blinked and shivered. "Did you just feel a cold wind come through here?"

"I did." Teresa arched an eyebrow in Charley's direction. "It felt like an evil spirit. We may need to do an exorcism."

Charley glared at Teresa. "Oh, that's right! Take his side. I thought you were my friend."

Teresa gave him an easy smile. Amanda felt certain the expression was every bit as forced as hers had been, but Teresa was much better at fake smiles than she was. Teresa got a lot of practice at parties when she was married to a wealthy entrepreneur/con artist. "This is such a wonderful evening, being with *friends*." She lifted her margarita and looked around the table, her gaze lingering on Charley for a long moment, assuring him he was included. "Here's to friends."

Amanda lifted her glass then took a large gulp of her margarita. Charley was not her friend. In life he had not been her friend. In death he certainly wasn't.

"Are you folks ready to order?" The waiter stood at Jake's elbow.

"Everybody agreed on steak fajitas for four?" Ross asked.

Everyone except Charley nodded. "Nobody cares what I'd like." He muttered a swear word then floated across the room and took an empty seat at a table with an older couple. "Hi, folks. Mind if I join you? Thank you, yes, I'd love a beer."

They continued eating, blissfully unaware of his presence.

If he went away to sulk at regular intervals, perhaps the evening wouldn't be a total disaster.

Jake handed both menus to the waiter then returned his attention to her. "How has your week been? Get any new motorcycles in for repair?"

"Well, a grungy looking guy who probably deals drugs in his spare time brought in a new BMW that has a tiny scratch, and an investment banker in a suit wants to have Vanson & Hines pipes added to his vintage Harley. How was your week? Find any new dead bodies?"

"Not even any old dead bodies," Jake said. "It's been a slow week for murders. We did nothing but eat doughnuts all week."

"Hey, don't forget that jay walker we hauled in and tortured for two days until he confessed." Ross laid his hand over Teresa's on the table top. "What about your week?"

She looked into his eyes as if torturing a jay walker was the sexiest thing she'd ever heard—or at least the man who claimed to have done it was the sexiest man she'd ever seen. "I talked to the spirit of a client's great grandfather who told him where he'd buried the family jewels worth ten million dollars."

Silence surrounded the table. Since Teresa actually did talk to spirits, her story could be true.

"Did you really?" Amanda asked.

An impish grin spread over Teresa's face. "No. But I did contact a woman's son who died of an overdose. He told his mother he's happy and he's not an addict anymore so that's sort of worth ten million dollars. Right?" She looked at Ross defiantly, daring him to contradict her. There could be no doubt Ross was attracted to Teresa, but he didn't seem entirely comfortable with her ability to talk to dead people.

"Yes," Amanda agreed. "It is." She leaned back and looked at Jake to see how he was taking the conversation. If he could deal with Teresa's ability, perhaps he could understand about Charley. If he couldn't, that didn't bode well for the future of their relationship.

His expression was unreadable. She could no more tell what he thought about talking to dead people than she could tell what secrets he and Ross were keeping about dead bodies or the lack thereof.

She reached for another tortilla chip and again his hand touched hers, evoking a warm, tingling sensation.

"Hey! Don't touch my wife!" Charley was back.

Amanda cringed and yanked her hand away.

"More chips and salsa." Their waiter leaned over the table between Jake and Ross, placed a fresh basket of chips in the center, and lifted a bowl of salsa from his tray.

Charley darted through the waiter. The man's eyes widened and his hands shook at the burst of cold. Charley spun and repeated the process, targeting the arm that held the salsa.

The waiter gasped and jerked backward…and the bowl of salsa fell into Jake's lap.

Amanda shot up from her chair. "I can't believe you did that!"

The waiter's face flamed bright red. "I'm so sorry."

"I didn't mean you." Amanda felt her own face glowing.

Jake sponged his crotch with his napkin. "It's okay. No problem."

He was wrong. There was a problem all right, a problem about six feet tall and slightly translucent.

Charley stood behind Jake, his arms folded, a smug expression on his face.

"I'm so sorry," the waiter repeated. "I will bring more napkins."

Amanda flopped onto her chair and clenched her fists. As soon as she got home, she was going to do an Internet search for ways to kill a ghost. She looked at Teresa, hoping the only other person who could see Charley would have some plan for banishing him. Teresa widened her eyes and shrugged helplessly. Amanda widened her eyes back. Surely Teresa could at least come up with something to gag him for the evening. Teresa gave a slight shake of her head.

Somehow they made it through the meal. Amanda felt certain the fajitas were wonderful, but with Charley capering around and through them periodically, she had to force down her food. He passed his chilly hands through Jake's beef. Jake looked surprised when the steaming steak strips stopped steaming, but he ate the cold meat without comment.

Amanda made a mental note of one more reason to punish Charley if she ever figured out how to do it.

Finally the meal was over. Much as she enjoyed spending time with Jake, Amanda was relieved. Now she only had to get through a movie which didn't require conversation. Charley would do his best to ruin that part of the evening too, but surely it wouldn't be as bad as dinner. Surely the horror had peaked and the evening couldn't get any worse.

"Anybody up for sopapillas?" Jake asked.

"I can't eat another bite," Amanda said. That was certainly true. Her stomach was full of knots, knots that would do any sailor proud.

Ross turned to Teresa. For once she wasn't looking at him. Her gaze was focused over his head. "He can't hear you, but I can," she said softly.

Amanda froze. Was Teresa talking to spirits in the middle of the restaurant, in the middle of the already disastrous evening?

"Who are you?" Teresa asked.

Apparently she was.

"I'll tell him," she said.

Ross and Jake both looked at her.

"I see him," Charley said. "He's looking at me. Hi! I'm Charley."

Amanda peered at Charley dubiously. Even though he was a spirit, he was on such a low level of that realm, he hadn't been able to see or interact with other spirits.

He couldn't lie, but he could be mistaken. If he wasn't lying, what did it mean? Was he moving up in the spirit world, getting ready to go into the light?

She took a second to check her feelings, to be sure she was ready for him to move on, that she wouldn't miss him even a little bit.

Nope. She was totally ready for him to go.

Teresa looked at Charley for a long moment, then her gaze shifted back to the live people at the table. "Ross, your brother's here with a message for you. He loves you and so do your parents, and then he said something about trust." She spread her hands. "Trusting you?"

"Trust fund!" Charley shouted. "He said Ross needs to check his trust fund."

Teresa glanced at Charley again, bit her lip and smiled at Ross. "Trust fund. Sorry I couldn't understand everything. It's so noisy in here."

Ross' facial muscles twitched in an expression somewhere between a smile and a frown. "You just talked to my...brother?"

She nodded. "He says his name is Parker."

"Yes!" Charley said. "I heard him say his name. I can see spirits now. Can you see me, Parker? He can see me! I can see him and he can see me. Wait, don't leave!" Charley darted across the room then darted back, his expression sad. "He went away before we got a chance to get to know each other."

Although Ross wasn't aware of the drama, his expression veered toward a frown. "My brother's name is Parker. How do you know that?"

"Your brother's spirit just visited you and asked me to pass on a message."

Ross arched an eyebrow. His lips twisted as if fighting a battle between smiling at a bad joke or frowning at a bad joke.

Teresa sat straighter, prepared for battle. "He looks a lot like you except his hair's longer and his shoulders aren't as broad. Younger?"

"That's him," Charley said. "That's who I saw. Think he's going to come back? I'd really like to talk to him."

Amanda held her breath as she waited for Ross to respond to Teresa.

"Yes, Parker is eight years younger. I thought you only talked to dead people."

Teresa's eyes widened. Her gaze darted from Amanda to Charley and back to Ross. "I do." She swallowed and ran her tongue over her lips. "He is. I mean…you didn't know?"

Ross' features hardened in disbelief. "I talked to my brother this morning. He's very much alive." But he didn't sound sure. He sounded scared. His tan face had gone pale.

"I'm sorry. He's not."

"He is."

"Maybe it just happened." Teresa's voice was barely audible. "Maybe that's why he went away so soon. He hasn't learned to control his movements."

Ross shook his head slowly, his lips compressed. He slid his cell phone from his pocket and hit a speed dial number. For a few seconds he waited, his gaze fixed on Teresa. Then he smiled. "Parker? Hello?" He pressed the phone more tightly to one ear and covered the other with his free hand. "I can't hear you. What's all the noise? Hello? Hello?"

The waiter returned to their table. "I spoke with my manager, and we will comp your meals. There will be no charge, and again I apologize for the accident."

Jake took money from his wallet and handed the waiter a tip. "Thank you."

Ross studied his uncooperative cell phone then tapped in a text message.

No one moved or spoke.

A long moment passed. Amanda exchanged a nervous glance with Teresa.

Ross' cell dinged. He held it up triumphantly so everyone could read the reply.

Sorry about the noise. I'm sitting in a bar with a hot chick when I should be home studying for geology test. How about you?

The color flowed back into Ross' face along with a mixture of anger and relief. "My brother is just fine."

Teresa looked confused. "I...I'm glad your brother is all right. I don't understand, but I'm glad I was mistaken."

Charley frowned. "What's wrong with Ross? The boy's dead. He was all see-through and floating a foot off the floor." Charley looked down at the location of his own feet and slowly settled to the floor.

Ross folded his napkin and turned to Teresa, but it wasn't the happy, flirtatious way he usually looked at her. His gaze was sober and a little sad. "I know you want me to believe in your ability, but this isn't the way to do it."

"But I..." Teresa bit her lip. For a moment Amanda thought she was going to cry. Instead she produced a smile and picked up her purse. "Well, shall we go?"

Amanda had thought the evening couldn't get any worse. It wasn't the first time she'd been wrong.

Chapter Two

Amanda climbed determinedly up the stairs to her apartment on the second floor over her motorcycle repair shop. Jake held her left arm and walked beside her. Charley floated through the rail on the right side, his icy grip never leaving her elbow, his monologue rolling on incessantly.

"What do you think it means that I could see Parker? I must be doing something right. Hey! Don't get so close to that man. I'm right here. I can see you. That was pretty cool, being able to see another spirit. I'd like to talk to him, exchange stories. Tell Detective Daggett to take his hand off your arm!"

Early winter swept through the night and wrapped chilly air around them. Or maybe it was just a reflection of how Amanda felt inside...cold and dark.

The movie had been violent and bloody, the short walk to their cars silent and tense. She had probably experienced a more awkward occasion sometime during her life but it was hard to recall just when. Maybe the Halloween party she'd attended dressed as a hooker because her date failed to tell her it was a church social. Or the literature class when she'd had to give an oral book report after reading half the book. At least that had only lasted an hour. The current event lasted six hours and felt like sixty.

"I think your friend upset Ross," Jake said.

Amanda flinched. "Yeah, that was obvious. He didn't like hearing that his brother's dead."

"Dead men don't answer phones and send text messages."

"I could if I wanted to," Charley said sullenly.

He might be right. In his current state of pure energy, he was able to turn on the television and make weird things happen to cell phones and computers.

"She really does see spirits of people who've died," Amanda said. "She saw my grandfather." *And Charley.* "Maybe Ross' brother's spirit somehow disconnected for a few minutes. Maybe he was doing meditation or something and his spirit left his body briefly."

"Meditating in a bar? Ross really likes Teresa, but that whole thing about seeing ghosts may be a problem."

Will it be a problem for us if I tell you I see my dead husband's ghost? Amanda swallowed the question. This was only their third date. Too soon for confessions. I *eat tortilla chips in bed, I have cold feet, I burp after my first Coke of the day, and my ex-husband's ghost lives with me.*

They reached the landing, turned and started up the final steps to her front door.

What would she do when they got to the door? At the end of the evening of the first two dates, she'd invited Jake in for a glass of wine. They sat and talked then shared long, delicious good night kisses. But those evenings Charley had been across town with Teresa, held hostage by the connection she'd accidentally forged with him while trying to cross him to the other side.

Tonight Teresa was with Ross, and Charley was with Amanda.

She shivered.

Jake wrapped his arm around her waist. "That breeze is cold. I think we're in for an early winter."

"Tell him to take his hands off you right now," Charley ordered. "If he doesn't, I'm going to be forced to do something."

What did Charley think he was going to do other than yell at her and make Jake shiver?

The three of them reached the top landing. Amanda took her keys from her purse.

Charley darted forward and stood in front of the door, arms outspread, attempting to block their entrance. "He's not coming in here."

She didn't want to give in to Charley's demands, but she didn't want to spend the evening being tortured by him either. She turned to face Jake, uncertain what to say.

He looked down at her, brown eyes warm, full lips slanted in a half smile. She desperately wanted to kiss those lips and feel those arms around her. Charley had been a good kisser, a skill which played a part in her decision to marry him since her former boyfriend had not. But Jake took that skill to a whole new level, made an art out of it, a delicious, seductive art.

As Jake's lips came closer, she decided she'd been wrong about the weather. She felt quite warm. She tilted her head and stretched toward him.

"No!" Charley rushed between them, a blast of frigid air.

Jake shivered and pulled back. "You get some cold winds up here on the second floor, don't you?"

"Yeah, sometimes it gets very chilly." She scowled at Charley who responded by darting through them again. "Uh..." *Ask Jake in and put up with Charley or send him away?*

Amanda's heart sank to her toes. She had no choice. This evening would definitely top the list of her worst experiences.

She lifted a hand to her forehead and prepared to drag out the overused excuse of a headache. Would he think she was trying to get rid of him? Would he feel rejected and never ask her out again? Would her fear that he'd reject her when he found out about Charley become a moot point?

Jake took her hand. "Are you feeling okay? You seemed a little off all evening."

He was giving her the perfect out.

Except she didn't want to take it.

"Get rid of him," Charley demanded.

That made her decision easier. Not only did she not want Jake to leave, but she refused to take orders from Charley. Somehow she'd get through the evening in spite of whatever interruptions he came up with.

"I feel fine, but it is cool outside. Why don't you come in and I'll make you a cup of hot chocolate?"

A slow smile tilted his luscious lips. "I'd like that."

Amanda stepped forward, reached through Charley and slid her key into the door then stopped. "It's unlocked. I could swear I locked it when we left."

Jake put his hands on her shoulders and moved her aside. "You did. I remember you doing it." His deep voice had changed from warm and sensual to grim and dangerous. He slid a gun from inside his jacket. He was in full cop mode. "Stay back."

For an irrational moment Amanda wondered if Ronald Collins had returned, was waiting in her apartment, high on drugs, ready to torture her.

But he was in jail awaiting trial, and besides, she'd put a bullet in his knee cap. He wasn't going anywhere without crutches for a long time.

Her breath caught in her throat. This wasn't Highland Park where she grew up. This was near Harry Hines Boulevard, a mixed bag of residences and businesses like the noisy bar down the street that catered to a rough crowd.

But her apartment was at the back of her motorcycle shop and up two flights of stairs. An unlikely target for burglars.

Unlikely but not impossible.

"I'll check the entire place while this dirt bag is wasting time playing Mr. Macho." Charley disappeared through the door.

Maybe the intruder would have a special bullet that could slay a ghost. If silver killed werewolves, surely some kind of metal could kill a ghost. Did they make bullets out of pyrite, fool's gold? That would be appropriate.

Jake eased the knob then kicked the door open. "Police!"

A high-pitched scream came from inside Amanda's apartment.

Charley rushed back through the door, a horrified expression on his face.

What terrible creature could horrify a ghost?

"It's your sister!"

"What?" Charley's words didn't make sense. Amanda only had one sister, and they were not close. Jenny was pregnant and was surely home with her lawyer husband *Davey* in their *cozy* house in Highland Park this late on a Saturday night.

She glanced behind her at the parking lot.

How had she failed to notice the white Mercedes sedan parked off to one side?

She'd been too enthralled with Jake.

"I'm unarmed!" a little girl voice shrieked.

Amanda stepped toward the open door. "Jenny?"

Jake stood in a classic Weaver stance, poised to shoot. He looked really hot that way, but one glance at the short, dark-haired, very pregnant woman in the middle of her living room doused all those thoughts even more effectively than Charley's presence did.

Jenny waddled toward her, and Jake stepped aside.

"I thought you'd never get home." Jenny wrapped her arms as far around Amanda as she could with her baby belly in the way.

"Uh..." With seven years difference in their ages and a thousand miles difference in their temperaments, the two had never been close. Certainly they'd never been affectionate toward each other or hugged each other. Until now.

Jenny burst into tears. "I've left him!"

Amanda patted Jenny on the back and stared at Jake. He holstered his gun and shrugged, looking as helpless as Amanda felt.

"Who have you left?" Surely not *Davey*, her soulmate.

"Davey's so mean to me!"

Mean? Amanda couldn't wrap her mind around the concept of Mean Davey. Perhaps he could be stern in dealing with tax matters for his clients, though she couldn't swear to that. For sure he was a total softie when dealing with his wife. "What did he do? Did he hit you?"

Jenny pulled away. "No, of course he didn't hit me. Why would you think something like that about Davey? Oh!" She turned toward Jake. "I didn't realize you had company." She extended a bare hand toward him. The glittering diamonds that usually covered her fingers were missing, and the hand looked surprisingly small and vulnerable. "I'm Jenny, Amanda's sister."

Amanda stepped forward. "Jenny, this is my, uh, friend, Jake. Jake, my sister, Jenny."

Jake's hand swallowed Jenny's in a brief shake. "Pleased to meet you, Jenny."

"Very nice to meet you, Jake. I'm so sorry to interrupt your evening."

Jake sidled toward the door. "No problem. You didn't interrupt anything. We were just saying goodnight. I'll call you tomorrow, Amanda."

She nodded. "Okay." Well, that took care of what she should do about him.

Jake opened the door and Amanda stepped over to close it behind him. He turned, leaned toward her and gave her a brief kiss, a quick peck. "Later," he whispered.

The kiss...the promise...was enough to lift her spirits.

"I saw that!" Speaking of spirits...

Amanda closed the door. She was alone with Jenny and Charley.

Again she'd been wrong about the evening not getting any worse.

Jenny once more burst into tears and sobbed on Amanda's shoulder. "You're so lucky you got rid of Charley before you got pregnant because it's not fun! Look how fat I am! I can't sleep at night and I have to go to the bathroom every few minutes and I can't wear my rings because my hands are swollen like a boxer's and I can't wear high heels because I'm unbalanced, and I need to wear high heels because I'm short! You know I've always worn heels so people would look up to me. You're tall. You don't have to worry about that, but I do, and I have lots of pretty shoes, and I can't wear any of them but it doesn't matter anyway because I can't wear any of my dresses that go with the shoes because I'm huge. I want this baby to get here so I can have my body back! I'm so glad you came home! I need my sister!"

That was really strange. Jenny was their mother's daughter. They had always been joined at the hip. Amanda was odd daughter out. Of course, Jenny was their mother's biological daughter and Amanda wasn't. Jenny was a clone of their mother, doing all the right things, following the rules while Amanda...didn't.

She patted Jenny's back in a futile attempt to soothe her. "What about Mother? Don't you need your mother at a time like this?" *Please say you need your mother. I don't know what to do with a sobbing, pregnant person.*

"She and Daddy are in Hawaii for some sort of award he's getting. Can you believe they left me alone at a time like this? I don't have anybody but you!"

"Oh, yes, the Hawaii trip. So if Davey didn't hit you, what did he do that's so bad you had to leave?"

Jenny wailed louder. "He's just awful! He does terrible things!"

"Like what?"

Jenny snuffled. "Well...I think he's cheating on me and why wouldn't he when I look like this?"

"Let's sit down and, uh, talk," Amanda suggested. "Maybe have some ice cream." Pregnant women craved ice cream, didn't they?

Jenny nodded and snuffled again. It was better than sobbing. "That would be nice. Ice cream just like when we were little girls and you'd get up in the middle of the night and sneak into the kitchen then come to my room and we'd sit on my bed and eat ice cream and talk."

Amanda didn't correct the pretty story by reminding Jenny how that evening ended with her sister spilling chocolate syrup on her bed and white carpet. The next day she'd sworn to their mother that Amanda had done it. Though Amanda had protested, it was the bad sister's word against the good sister's.

But they were adults now, not children.

Jenny waddled toward the sofa then plopped onto it with a sigh...next to her three designer suitcases.

"Omigawd!" Charley said. "I think she's moved in."

Three suitcases couldn't begin to hold all the possessions Jenny needed on a daily basis...but it was a scary start.

Jenny's gaze followed hers to the luggage. "I'd have put them in the guest room, but you don't have a guest room. Does Mother know you don't have a guest room?"

"Well, um, I don't think the subject's ever come up. She's never been here, so...probably not." Amanda looked around her apartment, the place she called home, the place she had furnished haphazardly from attics and garage sales, selecting each piece because it appealed to her but with no particular pattern in mind.

Suddenly, rather than seeing the room as a comfortable whole, everything split into disparate elements. The hardwood floors were in decent shape, protected through the years by the ugly green carpet she'd ripped out before moving in, but they were scuffed and needed polishing. The coffee table didn't match the lamp tables which didn't match the bookcase that loomed on one wall and held her books, old and new, all treasured. One lamp was a Tiffany style with only a couple of cracks in the brightly colored glass, and the other had an ordinary shade but a crystal base. They both gave out light. Her bulky nineteen inch television rested on a small bookcase in the corner of the room. Her sofa, the one item she'd purchased new, blazed with brilliant bursts of red, purple, yellow and green. It sort of matched the Tiffany style lamp. The eclectic, boisterous aura contrasted dramatically with her parents' and her sister's homes. They both had a quiet ambience and lamps that matched. And, as Jenny had pointed out, Amanda had no guest room.

This was the first time a family member had seen her place. It was the first time she'd seen it through their eyes. She expected Jenny to run screaming from the room to find the nearest hotel with a spa.

"Uh, Jenny..." She waved a hand around the room, unable to finish her sentence, biting back the irrational urge to apologize for living in a place she loved.

"I promise not to get in the way," Jenny said. "You won't even know I'm here."

Amanda blinked. "What?"

"I'll just sleep on the sofa." She patted the cushion next to her.

"Don't let her," Charley said. "You know I like to watch TV in here while you're sleeping."

"No!" Amanda was speaking to Charley but her sister's stricken expression told her she thought the denial was meant for her. "You can't sleep on the sofa. You'll be uncomfortable."

Jenny sighed. "I'm always uncomfortable. Just get me a pillow and a blanket, and I'll be fine. I'm short. I'll fit."

Amanda had bought the sofa because it was cheerful, not because it was comfortable. "Uh, you'd fit lengthwise, but..." She paused. Considering Jenny's rant about her size, it might not be a good idea to say the sofa was too narrow to accommodate her bulk. "It's really hard." She reached down and pushed on a cushion to demonstrate. "There are some very nice motels around here. I'll take you to one."

Charley sneered. "How? On the back of your motorcycle? She'll get her wish about that baby coming soon."

Jenny wiped her eyes with a hand that looked nude without her usual array of rings. "I don't want to go to a motel and be all alone. I want to stay with my sister. Please let me stay with you."

"Don't do it!" Charley ordered.

Charley's command sealed the deal. "Of course you can stay. But you're going to take the bed."

Jenny lifted her hands to her cheeks, tilted her head and smiled. "That's so sweet, but I can't let you do that. I'll be all right out here. I don't sleep much anyway."

"No way is my future niece going to sleep on the sofa. Besides, you said you have to go to the bathroom a lot, and my bathroom is in my bedroom. You sleep in there and that way you won't wake me when you get up to go."

"I am going to puke," Charley announced. "Have you ever seen ghost puke? It's not a pretty sight."

Jenny struggled to her feet and again wrapped her arms around Amanda's neck. "Thank you. You have no idea how much this means to me. I hope you're never in this situation, but if you are, I'll do the same for you, except I have a guest room." She stepped back and her blue eyes welled with tears again. "I used to have a guest room. Now Davey has my guest room. I don't know where the baby and I will live, probably in some hovel."

"About that ice cream," Amanda interrupted. "Chocolate or vanilla?"

Jenny clapped her hands together. "Vanilla with chocolate sauce and nuts."

"Sorry, no nuts."

"There's one nut here," Charley said.

Two. Maybe three. She had just given her bed to Jenny and volunteered to sleep on her uncomfortable sofa.

Chapter Three

Jenny devoured her ice cream and looked on longingly as Amanda added a large glass of wine to her late night snack. Rude to drink it in front of somebody who couldn't have wine, but it was a little rude of that person to invite herself over for the night. Any tiny speck of guilt Amanda might have felt vanished along with the last drop of her wine. She felt mellow and calm in spite of her sister's presence.

Jenny toddled off to bed and Amanda brought sheets, a blanket and a pillow to the sofa then lay down on it. Not so bad. She didn't dare roll over for fear of falling off, but at least it was long enough she could stretch out, and the wine increased the comfort level.

The biggest problem was that Jenny was still talking. The baby might be stretching her stomach and making her uncomfortable, but nothing interfered with her ability to talk. The bedroom and living room were next to each other, and Jenny had left the connecting door open.

"I don't know how I'm going to take care of this baby all alone. I've heard about single moms and how hard it is for them."

"You'll be fine. Mother will help you."

"I wanted to name this baby after mother, but Davey wanted to name her after his grandmother. He said we should compromise. His grandmother's name is Doris. Can you imagine? Beverly Doris?" She hiccupped a sob. "I'm the one having this baby so you'd think I could at least name her after my own mother and now I'm going to have to raise her by myself and I don't know anything about being a mother."

"Yeah, I guess babies don't come with an instruction manual. But you'll be fine. Remember when we used to play with dolls? You were always so much more maternal than I was."

Jenny giggled. "Remember how mad Mother got when you said my dolls robbed a bank and you hanged them?"

The hanging had been going quite nicely until Jenny ran crying to their mother. But that was long ago and far away. "Everything's going to be all right," Amanda assured her. And it would be. Either Jenny would go back to her husband or home to her mother who would be back from Hawaii in a few days. She'd have the baby, hire a nanny and return to playing bridge. "Get some sleep and everything will look better in the morning."

Jenny was quiet for a few minutes, and Amanda drifted into the soothing, incoherent world of sleep.

"It feels like I've been pregnant all my life." The words jerked Amanda back to full consciousness. "I don't even remember what my toes look like. Don't ever get pregnant, Amanda."

Amanda didn't think she had to worry about that as long as Charley was around. Latest birth control device. Her ex-husband's jealous ghost.

"...and Davey's talking about having another baby when we haven't even had this one yet. I don't want to ever be like this again but this one's a girl and he wants a boy. Mother and Daddy didn't have any boys, and they're doing just fine. Why do men think they have to have a son to make their life complete?"

"Can't you make her shut up?" her birth control device complained. "Your sister has always got on my nerves, but now I can't even go down to the bar to get away from her like I did when I still had a body."

"Isn't that just too bad that you can't escape to the bar?"

"What?" Jenny asked. "Escape to the bar? Why would I want to escape to the bar? I can't drink. I'm pregnant. I haven't had a glass of wine for months. That wine you were drinking looked so good."

"That wine came in a box. You wouldn't have liked it. What I said was, too bad having a baby is so hard. You really should try to get some sleep. You're sleeping for two now."

"Oh." Jenny was silent for a moment as if considering the absurd comment. "I didn't think of it that way. Okay."

Beautiful silence. In the distance a dog barked. A mockingbird gave a short trill. Normal sounds of the night, sounds Amanda could sleep with.

She pulled the blanket to her chin and closed her eyes.

"Do you think I'll ever fit into a size two again? I can't imagine I ever will. Marcia Benton told me I'll have to exercise but I don't like to exercise. It makes you sweaty and tired and it's boring. I've got to go to the bathroom again. I'll never get any sleep if I can't stay out of the bathroom."

The floor creaked. Jenny groaned.

"We're not going to get any sleep either," Charley said.

"You don't sleep."

"No, I don't," Jenny said. "If I'm not going to the bathroom, the baby's kicking. I have no idea how somebody so small can kick so hard. I've seen her picture on the sonogram, and she's tiny. The doctor says she's fine, that's she's small because I'm so small, but I'm not small anymore."

The toilet flushed and the plumbing groaned.

Amanda had become accustomed to the sounds of the old plumbing, but now it grated on her nerves, sounded loud enough for the patrons at the bar down the block to hear it. And Jenny had said she would be going to the bathroom several times during the night.

"Here's the plan," Charley said. "I'll distract her while you throw a sheet over her, then we'll drag her downstairs, put her in her fancy car, take her home, and dump her on the front porch."

Amanda wasn't sure how Charley planned to distract her, but his crazy plan didn't sound all that bad. Jenny needed to leave. Maybe Amanda could light a candle under the smoke detector or shoot off a gun and claim they were being bombed.

"Oh!" A soft touch on her arm startled her.

Jenny stood beside the sofa. "It means so much to me that you're taking me in like this. If you ever get pregnant, I'll be there for you. I'm so glad we have each other. How terrible if we were only children. You're my sister, and I love you."

"Oh, gag," Charley said.

Amanda glared at him, took Jenny's hand and squeezed it. "I love you too. Maybe a cup of hot chocolate would help you sleep."

"With whipped cream?"

"No whipped cream. Sorry." Amanda got up and headed toward the kitchen. Jenny could have hot chocolate and she'd have another glass of wine.

Jenny plopped onto the sofa and sighed. "It's okay. I can skip the whipped cream. I don't need the extra calories. This baby only weighs five and a half pounds, so I don't know how they can say I'll be thin again when she's born. I've gained twenty pounds. Well, twenty-two, to be exact. So I'll still be seventeen pounds overweight, and I'm so short, I can't carry that much extra weight. You're lucky you're tall like Daddy. I got Mother's height and her hair. Straight as a string. Mother says you got your curly red hair from Daddy's grandfather. He doesn't look like he has red hair, but all those pictures are black and white, so it's hard to tell."

Amanda made hot chocolate while her sister talked. What had her sister said was the problem? That she thought Davey was cheating on her? Her own experience proved it was impossible to predict who'd have an affair, but Davey seemed an unlikely candidate. He was so reserved, Amanda was amazed the two of them had actually created a baby.

More likely Jenny was suffering from a surfeit of hormones and would be back to normal when the baby was born. Well, normal for her. In the meantime, it was too bad she didn't have some Ambien to slip into Jenny's hot chocolate.

கூக

Amanda struggled to wakefulness at the sound of birds and wind chimes. The ring tone had seemed a good idea at the time, but this morning it was annoying. She hadn't got much sleep and she knew for a fact that Jenny hadn't either.

She snatched her cell phone off the coffee table, half expecting to find Jenny calling from the bedroom.

Teresa's picture appeared on the display.

She accepted the call. "Good morning."

"Amanda, are you alone?"

Amanda sighed and pushed her hair back from her face. "No, I'm not alone. My apartment's actually quite crowded, but Jake's not here, if that's what you're asking. What's going on? What time is it?"

"Ten o'clock. I waited as long as I could because I thought maybe...well, obviously not."

"Hi, Teresa!" Charley said. "That was pretty exciting last night, right? Both of us talking to spirits."

"Hello, Charley. Amanda, can you come over? I need to talk to somebody. It's about Ross' brother."

"Ross' brother? The undead one?"

"Oh, he's dead."

Not a good start to the day. "Well, my sister's here. Maybe you could come over—no, never mind. Give me fifteen minutes to shower and I'll start your way."

"Thank you."

Amanda disconnected the call and headed through the bedroom door to the bathroom. Jenny was still sleeping. After the restless night both of them had, she didn't want to wake her.

But when she finished her shower and came out, Jenny was awake and sitting on the side of the bed. "Good morning, sister of mine. Let's go down to the Kozy Kitchen and get some breakfast, my treat. I'm ready for one of their wonderful omelets. Carrying this baby around all the time is a lot of work." She grasped the iron bed frame and pulled herself to her feet.

"I'd love to, but I'm on my way to visit my friend Teresa."

"Oh, girl talk! Sounds like fun! We can take her along for breakfast. Just give me a few minutes to get dressed. It takes me longer now." She sighed. "Everything takes longer. I've turned into such a slug. Even if I could go faster...and I can't because I'm so big...I worry all the time that I'll fall or something and hurt the baby. You have no idea how scary it is to be responsible for somebody's life, somebody you can't even see."

If Teresa needed to talk about communicating with dead people and Jenny was worried about hurting her baby, taking Jenny along would probably not be a good idea.

"I'm sorry, but Teresa's having a meltdown, and she doesn't want to see anybody but me."

Jenny made a sad face. "Oh, bless her heart. What's wrong? I'll talk to her. I have a lot of experience comforting people who have problems. People say I should be a counselor because I'm so good at it. Maybe I can get a degree in psychology and support my baby when I'm a single mom." She waddled toward the bathroom. "I'll just take a quick shower and be right with you, but we can't go on that awful motorcycle of yours. I'm driving my Mercedes. It's got the most comfortable ride of all our cars and, believe me, there's nothing comfortable about being pregnant." She disappeared into the bathroom, her words muted behind the closed door.

Amanda dashed to her closet, yanked on blue jeans and motorcycle gear, then waited a moment until she heard the sound of the shower. She opened the bathroom door and leaned in. "Jenny, I just talked to Teresa, and she appreciates your offer, but she would be too humiliated to talk if anybody else was there!"

"You told a lie," Charley accused.

"I have a good teacher."

Jenny poked her head out of the shower. "Amanda—"

"Help yourself to anything you find in the kitchen."

"You don't have anything in the kitchen but ice cream, a carton of Cokes, a package of Oreos, and some moldy cheese," Charley protested. "Your sister's always talking about eating her greens, and the only green thing you have is that cheese."

Amanda darted through the front door and down the stairs. "Moldy cheese won't hurt her. Nobody dies from eating blue cheese and it's moldy."

❧❧

Teresa was waiting with dark circles under her eyes, a fresh Coke in her hand and an agitated expression on her face. She offered the Coke to Amanda. "I figured you wouldn't have time for breakfast."

"Her sister wanted her to go to Kozy Kitchen." Charley entered Teresa's apartment and looked around the room. "Parker's not here."

"Not at the moment. He said he had to check on someone but he'd be right back. Trust me, he'll be back." Teresa closed the door behind them. "I'm sorry to take you away from your guest."

"It's okay." Amanda sank onto the white sofa amidst Teresa's collection of colorful pillows.

Charley sat beside her. "Yeah, she doesn't like her sister very much."

"Charley! I love her. She's my sister. She's just pregnant and hormonal and a little irritating right now."

"She was a whole lot irritating even when she wasn't pregnant," he said.

Teresa reached down to the coffee table, picked up a mug with a colorful fractal design, and took a seat in the white chair facing Amanda. Clutching the cup between both hands, she leaned forward. "Ross' brother has been here since I got home last night. The man is dead, stone cold dead. No doubt about it."

"If he's dead, who answered Ross' phone call? Who sent him the text message?"

"I asked him that."

Amanda leaned forward. "And?"

"He said it wasn't him, and it's not important who it was."

Amanda sat back. "That's a strange thing to say. You'd think he'd be outraged that someone was impersonating him."

"We've only begun on the strange stuff. Just because I happen to have the ability to talk to dead people, he thinks it's my responsibility to convince Ross that he's dead."

Amanda flinched. "Your efforts didn't go over so well last night."

"I know." Teresa shuddered. "Ross was pretty upset. He didn't even come inside with me. Said he was going home to call his brother. Why couldn't I have been born with a talent for singing or painting or anything but talking to spirits?"

"Blow him off," Charley advised. "You don't want some guy who treats you like that."

Teresa frowned at Charley. "I don't want to blow him off. I..." She lifted her chin defiantly. "I care about him."

"You know he's just a cop," Charley said. "He doesn't have any money."

Amanda looked around for a hole to crawl into. Teresa had been raised with money, then her family lost everything. She'd married a financially successful man and enjoyed the lifestyle until he tried to set her up for murder. Amanda had wondered more than once where an underpaid cop fit into her dreams, but she'd never been rude enough to say it.

Death hadn't improved Charley's tact.

"Ross will figure out soon enough that you're right about his brother and then he'll accept your talent as genuine." Amanda wasn't at all sure about that, but this was no time for a reality check.

The former cheerleader looked insecure and small. "What if he doesn't?"

Charley moved through the coffee table and laid a hand halfway through Teresa's shoulder in a semblance of a gesture of consolation. "Then you're better off without him."

"Charley!" Amanda snapped. "Enough! Of course things are going to work out between Ross and Teresa. You're being selfish because you don't like sharing her attention."

Charley's mouth twisted as he tried to tell a lie, to deny Amanda's accusation. Finally he returned to Amanda's side, folded his arms and sulked.

Sulking was good. Maybe she and Teresa could get something accomplished without his constant interruptions. "So tell me about this recent visit with Ross' brother. Parker? Is that his name?"

"Parker Romano Minatelli. Named after his maternal and paternal grandfathers. Hello, Parker. Welcome back." Teresa gestured toward the big screen TV above the fireplace. "Amanda, meet Parker. He likes to hang out around electronic things. Says it makes it easier to reach me."

Charley darted close to the TV. "And I'm Charley Randolph." He extended a hand then raised it up and down as if shaking with someone. That was a little creepy.

"Uh, pleased to meet you, Parker," Amanda said. "I guess I'm the only one here who can't see you."

"He says he's sorry, but he doesn't know how to make himself any more visible," Teresa said.

"It's okay. One ghost in my life is enough."

Teresa grimaced. "I should be so lucky. Okay, what we have to discuss is that Parker was murdered—"

Amanda almost choked on her Coke. "Murdered? By who?"

"He won't tell me. He says it's not important. What's important is that he wants me to lead Ross to his body so he can be declared dead."

Amanda took another drink of Coke, drawing out the action to give her time to take in everything and think about it. "Well, if you find his body, that will certainly prove...uh...that he's dead and you were right."

"Yeah, but taking Ross to his brother's lifeless body isn't likely to give him warm, fuzzy feelings about me." She ran a hand through her sleek hair and stared at the blank television screen. "I understand it's important, Parker, and I understand I'm the only one who can do it." She paused for a moment, listening. "Yes, I know it isn't easy for you to come through."

"It's easy for me," Charley said. "Maybe I could give you some pointers."

Teresa glowered at Charley then rose and headed toward the kitchen. "I need more coffee. I didn't sleep much last night. Do you know what it's like having a ghost talking to you all night?"

"As a matter of fact, I do. Would you bring me another Coke?" Amanda called after her. "I didn't sleep much last night either."

"Neither did I," Charley said. "Your sister even talks in her sleep."

Teresa returned from the kitchen with a steaming cup of coffee and a fresh Coke. She handed the Coke to Amanda and resumed her seat.

Amanda took a drink then set her can on the coffee table between the crystal bowl filled with colored gems and the deck of Tarot cards. She folded her hands. "Okay, let's do this. Call Ross and tell him."

Teresa grimaced. "Call him? Now?"

"Yes, now. If you don't, you may have your own personal version of Charley following you everywhere, nagging at you incessantly."

"Hey!" Charley protested, but he didn't deny anything.

Teresa set her mug on the lamp table and picked up her cell phone then hesitated and licked her lips.

She was usually so poised and self-confident. She really was concerned about Ross' reaction. How ironic would it be if she genuinely cared about a cop who'd never have enough money to support her in the lifestyle she craved?

Teresa hit a speed dial number then put the phone on speaker.

The number rang so long, Amanda thought it would go to voice mail.

"Hi, Teresa." Ross sounded pleased that she was calling.

"Hi."

"Listen, I'm sorry about last night."

Amanda relaxed. That was a good start.

"Yeah, me too," Teresa said.

"I guess I kind of overreacted. Parker's the only family I've got left. Our parents are dead. The thought that he might be dead…"

So much for the good start.

Teresa's expression sagged. She sent Amanda a silent appeal for help.

Amanda spread her hands in a helpless gesture.

Teresa cleared her throat and squirmed. "Well, Ross, you see..." She looked away. "Can we just forget it ever happened?"

Amanda sucked in her breath.

Charley's forehead creased in surprise. "Aren't you going to tell him the guy's dead?"

"Sh-h-h!" Amanda hissed then realized how silly she was being. Ross couldn't hear Charley. "You just want them to break up," she whispered. "Hush!"

Amanda turned back to Teresa who was gazing at the television and gritting her teeth.

"...glad we talked about it," Ross said.

That sentiment probably wasn't going to last long.

Teresa was silent for a moment then drew in a deep breath and released it in a long sigh. "All right, all right! I'll do it!"

"Do what?" Ross asked.

"I'm not talking to you. I meant...oh, damn. It's your brother again."

A heavy silence crashed through the phone.

Teresa groaned and her shoulders drooped. "I don't want to do this. Ross, your brother is here with me, and he's very insistent that I take you to his body so you can have him declared legally dead."

So much for that relationship. Teresa wouldn't have to worry about being involved with a man who couldn't support her.

Chapter Four

It could have been a romantic Sunday drive in early fall. Two couples motoring through the countryside. Beautiful, warm day. Green, gold and red leaves swirled in a colorful palette against the bright blue sky.

The small fact that Jake and Ross were both wearing denim jackets to hide their guns and the four of them were looking for a corpse took a lot of the romance out of the excursion.

Since Amanda sat next to Jake in the back seat of Ross' sedan, she might still have been able to derive some pleasure from his nearness had Charley not perched determinedly between them, his trademark cold infusing her shoulder.

In the front seat Ross kept his attention focused on the road ahead, and Teresa spoke only to give occasional terse directions. The silence between them was thick and bleak with none of their usual relaxed, flirtatious banter.

Ross didn't want to believe his brother was dead, murdered by person or persons unknown, his body dumped in the middle of nowhere. When Teresa told him Parker had not been the one who answered his phone call or sent the text message from his phone and he wouldn't say who did, any credibility she had left went straight down the drain.

He and Jake had arrived at Teresa's shortly after she'd blurted out that Parker wanted his body found so he could be declared dead. Ross said he'd brought Jake along *in the unlikely event we find something that requires the presence of a police officer.* Amanda suspected he needed a friend for moral support, and she suspected Jake and Teresa knew that too but they all went along with the official explanation and let him maintain his macho image.

As they drove deeper into the middle of nowhere, it became apparent why Parker hadn't been able to give them directions but insisted he must lead them to his body. Unless he'd been able to supply exact latitude and longitude, even a GPS would be worthless out here.

Go ten or so miles down a gravel road until you get to the big live oak tree then turn left on the dirt road. Which big live oak tree? The one with green leaves? Yes, that would be the one. Oh, they all have green leaves. Then continue past the twentieth chuckhole...or maybe it's the twenty-first.

"Turn right," Teresa instructed.

Ross slowed to a stop. "Turn right where? I don't see a road."

"There." She pointed through the brush. "He says there's a trail, and if we had a four wheeler, we could get through easily. That's how he came in. But since we don't, we have to walk."

Ross studied her in silence for a long moment then pulled the car as far off the road as possible. He was no longer arguing with Teresa or denying her assertions, but he was upset and dubious.

Wearing motorcycle boots and jeans, Amanda stepped out into knee high weeds. Teresa slid out into the same weeds in her sandals and khaki shorts. She forced a smile. "Parker forgot to tell me we were going hiking."

"He didn't think to mention it because things like that don't matter to us spirits." Charley glided several inches above the weeds.

Jake walked beside Amanda and took her hand. She wanted to smile at him, but Charley hadn't yet noticed the intimacy and she didn't want to draw his attention to it. She settled for squeezing Jake's hand while keeping her eyes straight ahead.

The five of them started down the poorly defined tracks through the weeds. Mesquite and oak trees still held green foliage while other trees were shedding red, gold, and brown leaves in a bright carpet. The landscape was transitioning from summer to winter, from vibrant and alive to sleeping. A bit like Ross and Teresa's relationship.

They were not holding hands. Sometimes the two of them were almost embarrassing with their public displays of affection. Not today. Their relationship had taken a nosedive straight from summer to winter, and there was no sign of spring.

Ghosts could do that to a relationship.

"We keep going until we come to an old well." Teresa's words were clipped and chilly.

As they trekked through the countryside, Amanda wondered if this was a wild goose chase or, in this case, a bogus corpse chase. Teresa wouldn't lie about something like this, but she could be wrong. Or maybe the spirit was lying to her. Just because Charley couldn't lie didn't mean the same rules applied to other spirits. Maybe this wasn't even Ross' brother. Teresa had never seen the man before so she could be mistaken. How would that affect her relationship with Ross? Probably not good. Find Parker's body and prove she was right, find a stranger's body and admit she was wrong…either way Teresa was in trouble.

The uneven ground covered with rocks, dead leaves, grass and a few trees stretched before them with no change. "Can you ask him how much farther?"

"He isn't sure. He was confused on his journey out here. It was dark and he still thought he was alive. He didn't understand what was going on. But he thinks we're getting close."

"Your killer sure did pick a tough place to get to," Charley complained. "Mine left me lying on my living room floor. Made it easier for Amanda to find me. I guess it was easier for him too. No body to lug around."

Amanda had no idea how or if Parker responded to Charley's comments. They continued walking in silence, the only sounds those of nature—occasional bird calls and the crunching of their footsteps as they walked through the fallen leaves and crisp grass.

An explosion burst through the quiet afternoon.

"Gunshot!" Jake dropped Amanda's hand, produced a gun, and flung the other arm in front of Amanda. "Get down!"

A gun magically appeared in Ross' hand. "I think it came from over there."

Always with the cop thing.

And sometimes...like now with a shot echoing through the countryside...that could be a good thing, a reassuring thing.

Jake looked back. "Get down!" he said, more imperatively this time.

If she got down, she wouldn't be able to see what was happening.

Jake and Ross ran in the direction of the gunshot.

"I'll go check it out," Charley volunteered. "I'm a lot faster than those clumsy cops." He sped ahead of everybody.

Amanda started to follow but Teresa laid a hand on her arm.

"Maybe we should stay here." Her face had gone a couple of shades paler than normal. Nothing to match Charley's ghostly pallor but getting close to Amanda's redhead skin.

"Why?"

Teresa raised both eyebrows. "Uh...gunshot? You don't think maybe that's enough reason to wait while the guys with guns check it out?"

"You talk to dead people, but you're frightened by a shot in the distance?"

Teresa clasped her hands. "Yes. I don't want to join those dead people just yet."

Amanda sighed. "Don't you watch horror movies? Now that the guys are gone, the monster will come up behind us and slit our throats if we stay here. Come on!" She took Teresa's arm and urged her forward.

Teresa came but not without protest. "Do you have any idea how uncomfortable these sandals are and how scratched my legs are?"

"It was your choice to dress sexy instead of comfortable. Hurry."

Amanda strode determinedly after Jake and Ross but slowed her pace when she noticed Teresa wasn't keeping up.

Another shot cracked the air.

Teresa gasped.

Amanda didn't break stride. "It's Texas in the fall. Probably deer hunters."

"Deer season's not open yet," Teresa protested.

"Yeah, and everybody obeys that law just like you obey the speeding laws."

A third shot.

If it was deer hunters, that deer was either dead or long gone.

Charley flashed to Amanda's side. "It's the men who killed Parker! They've got rifles! Run!"

Teresa gasped. "Parker's killers? How do you know?"

"Police! Drop your weapons!" A few feet ahead, Jake and Ross stood in shooter's stances, aiming their guns at someone. Was Charley right? Had Parker led them to his murderer?

"What the hell?" a deep voice protested.

Amanda left Teresa behind and hurried to catch up to Jake.

In a clearing just ahead two large, bearded men wearing baseball caps were carefully laying their rifles on the ground.

"What were you shooting at?" Jake demanded.

"Targets." The taller of the two men flung a hand outward.

Amanda peered in the direction he indicated and saw a bullet riddled target with the image of a zombie.

"Old man Carstairs call you again?" The second man, the shorter one with the larger paunch, scowled, bushy eyebrows almost meeting across his nose.

"Why would he have reason to do that?" Ross asked.

The taller man muttered an expletive. "That old coot. Yeah, we know this is his land." He smiled, his teeth surprisingly white in the middle of the scruffy brown beard. "We just wanted to get in a little practice before deer season starts next month, but we didn't want to scare the deer off our land. It's not like Carstairs hunts his property or lets anybody else. Deer just going to waste. No harm in running them over to our place." He winked.

"You boys got any ID on you?" Jake asked.

"Sure do. You show me yours, I'll show you mine."

Holding his gun steady with one hand, Jake reached into his pocket with the other, pulled out his wallet and flashed his badge. "Your turn."

The tall man smiled again. "No problem, officer. You can't blame us for being careful out here in the middle of nowhere when two men got guns pointed at us."

As the bearded men reached into their back pockets, Jake and Ross tensed.

The men brought out their wallets and extracted driver's licenses.

Jake strode over and checked out the one held by the taller man. "Stanley Wagner." He reached for the other man's. "And Clyde Wagner. You boys brothers?"

"Yep," Stanley replied. "Next farm over. Been there for five generations. You officers like to hunt? Get you a little fresh venison? Nothing better than venison chili on a cold winter night. We can make that happen. We lease this place to deer hunters every year. For you boys who keep the peace, we can waive the fee. Just a little thank you for all you do."

Jake handed back the licenses and dropped his arm to his side though he kept his fingers wrapped around the grips of his 9mm. "Appreciate that, but we do most of our hunting in the grocery store."

"Let me know if you change your mind. We might even arrange something a little early." Another sly wink.

"Why don't you boys call it a day for target practice? Go home before Mr. Carstairs decides to press charges for trespassing."

"You got it, officer," Clyde said. "You have a good day now, y'hear? And if you change your mind about the venison..."

49

Jake nodded and stepped back to join Ross. "I know where to find you."

They watched as the men retrieved their battered target and disappeared through the trees.

Ross looked at Teresa and burst into laughter. "Dorothy, we're not in Dallas anymore."

Amanda turned her attention to her pale, wide-eyed friend.

Teresa gave a shaky smile then a shaky laugh. "I thought those men were going to shoot you."

Ross grinned. "That's always a possibility, but we try to shoot them before they shoot us."

The incident had been unsettling, but it had broken Ross' grim detachment.

He laid his hand on Teresa's slender arm and she gazed up at him with the familiar gaga expression.

Amanda released a soft sigh and relaxed.

Charley snorted.

Jake cleared his throat. "Now that we've made the area safe for deer, maybe we should continue the search before it gets dark."

Ross' expression became grim once more but he continued to hold Teresa's arm protectively as they again plunged through the underbrush, getting back to the poorly-defined tracks.

Teresa suddenly stopped. "Where?" She moved to her left a couple of feet and stopped again. Ross did not follow.

She leaned over to examine something on the ground then straightened and turned to face Ross. Moisture swam in her dark eyes. "I'm sorry."

Ross tensed, his body woodenly straight.

Amanda drew in a sharp breath. What had Teresa found in the leaves? Parker's body? She moved toward her friend.

Charley was there first. He patted Teresa's shoulder. "Are you okay? I don't see a dead man."

If Amanda hadn't met Charley's parents and found them to be kind, caring people, she'd have thought he was raised by wolves. Ill-mannered wolves.

She brushed past Teresa and looked down. A hole in the ground approximately four feet in diameter surrounded by rocks placed there a long time ago and worn smooth with the passage of time and the elements.

A well. Teresa had said they would come to an old well.

Jake moved up beside her and produced a flashlight.

"No," Ross croaked. "Let me look first."

"Why don't I—" Jake began.

"No." Ross took the flashlight, strode over and squatted in the weeds surrounding the opening.

The wind fell to absolute stillness. No bird called. No leaf stirred. Amanda held her breath, afraid if she dared to breathe, it would sound like a hurricane.

Ross held the flashlight as far down in the opening as he could and moved it slowly back and forth.

Maybe his brother's body wasn't in the well.

Maybe Teresa was wrong...horribly, wonderfully wrong.

Amanda arched an eyebrow in Charley's direction. He'd insisted on being first on the scene to figure out who the shooters were. He could easily go down the well and have a look.

"I'm not going in there," he said. "I have claustrophobia." He shivered and wrapped ghostly arms about himself.

Teresa knelt beside Ross and put an arm around his shoulders. "Ross? Are you okay?"

He drew in a long breath and rose slowly. Shadows from the sun sinking low on the horizon slanted across his face, turning it to a mask of pain. He opened his mouth as if to speak, closed it, then cleared his throat. "I don't know if Parker's down there, but there's definitely a body. In fact, there appears to be more than one."

Chapter Five

Jake reached for the flashlight. Ross held onto it, knuckles turning white, face set in hard, resolute lines as if refusing to let anyone else see what was in the well would make it not true. Teresa moved quietly to his side and slid her fingers over his where they gripped the barrel of the flashlight. He scowled at her for a moment then dropped his head and let go.

Jake took the light, knelt on the ground and peered into the opening.

An invisible force seemed to suck all the light and sound from the world around them. Ross leaned close to Teresa as if for support, but he didn't look at or touch her.

Amanda held her breath again.

Even Charley was silent.

Jake rose, his expression unreadable, dusted off the knees of his jeans and cleared his throat. "We need to get in touch with the authorities. Out this far, it's probably going to be the Kraken County Sheriff's Department." He spoke matter-of-factly as though the tone of his voice could negate whatever he'd seen in the dark depths.

Ross took out his cell phone. "I don't have any bars."

Jake pulled his phone from his pocket and shook his head. "Me neither."

"Mine's back in the car," Teresa said.

"Mine's..." Amanda hesitated, trying to recall the last time she'd seen her cell phone. On the coffee table in her apartment. She'd left in such a hurry, she'd forgotten it. Not that she expected to have reception if nobody else did.

"I'll go back to the car," Ross said, "find the sheriff or whoever, while you all stay here and, uh, guard the crime scene."

"Like somebody's going to stroll by and contaminate it?" Amanda asked.

Ross' gaze dropped to Teresa's scratched legs and battered sandals.

Ah. That was his concern. "Which could certainly happen with crazy men like those hunters we just saw," Amanda added quickly.

"You stay here," Jake said. "I'll go."

Ross looked as if he was going to argue but shook his head and mumbled, "All right."

If his brother's body was in the well, he probably wanted to stay close.

Maybe he wanted to stay there and watch over Teresa.

Jake nodded, turned and set off in the direction they'd come.

"Jake and Ross should both go," Charley said. "Then the four of us can hang out and talk while they're gone."

Teresa narrowed her eyes at Charley and gave a slight shake of her head. "Thank you, Jake."

"I should go with you." Amanda followed on his heels. Enforced time alone together might be a good thing for Teresa and Ross.

"No!" Charley, Ross, Jake and Teresa protested. Only Charley sounded as though he meant it, and his opinion didn't count.

Amanda caught up to Jake and matched his strides through the underbrush. "You'll probably need my guidance to get back to the car."

"I was a boy scout. I have a very good sense of direction."

"That's great because I don't."

Jake kept walking. "I know you don't. I also know you're trying to help them by leaving them alone. If they're going to have any chance, she needs to ease up on that ghost stuff."

"Hey!" Charley protested. "Wait till he's dead. Then he'll have a different idea about *that ghost stuff*."

But in the intervening years...hopefully a lot of intervening years...Amanda needed Jake to accept the presence of spirits. She didn't think she could keep Charley a secret forever. "If you don't believe she really talks to spirits, how do you explain finding the well with the dead bodies?" Amanda asked, stretching her strides to keep up as they plunged through the underbrush. She had long legs, but Jake's were longer.

"We don't know for sure Ross' brother's body is in that well."

"Yeah, right. It's just a coincidence that Teresa led us to a dead body. How would she know where to look if she didn't have some kind of help?"

Jake stopped abruptly and turned back to her, his expression grim. "That's a very good question. The authorities will probably want to know the answer to that, and I don't think they're going to buy into her ghost story." He turned away. "We need to hurry. It's going to be dark soon."

Amanda dashed after him. "Wait! What are you saying? That they may think Teresa killed somebody?"

"Teresa wouldn't kill anybody," Charley said. For once they were in agreement.

"Jake! You know that's not true." She rushed forward, reaching for his shoulder to halt him, hit him...something. Her foot struck a rock hidden in the leaves and she stumbled, falling into the brittle debris of autumn.

Jake spun around. "Amanda!" He reached for her, but she was already struggling to her feet and ignored his proffered hand. "Are you hurt?"

"I'm fine." She'd landed painfully on one knee but wasn't about to admit that to someone who could suspect her friend of murder.

He took her hands in his and looked at her palms then at her face.

"Hey!" Charley protested.

She twisted away from Jake's warm fingers. "No blood. Let's go before it gets dark."

Jake's gaze lingered for a moment, intense and probing, then he nodded and turned back to the path.

They'd trekked through the woods and found dead bodies, maybe Ross' brother. Ross was not happy with Teresa and would probably be even more unhappy if one of the bodies was his brother. Teresa could be a murder suspect. The sun was sinking low on the horizon and it would likely be dark when they made the return journey to the bodies. And, oh, yeah, Charley was always there and her very pregnant sister was waiting back at her apartment.

Was there anything good about this day?

"I don't like the way he held your hands," Charley grumbled. "That's just not right when your husband is standing here watching him."

Nope. Not one thing good about the whole stinking day. And all the problems except her sister were a direct result of ghosts.

☜☞

The journey back to the well was faster and easier. The sheriff and his deputy arrived in a large truck and unloaded two four-wheelers. Small carts attached to each of them contained an impressive amount of equipment. When they set off into the woods, the sheriff rode one vehicle with Jake on the back, and Amanda rode with the deputy on the other one. Neither man had been pleased to have their Sunday evening interrupted, but the promise of a well full of dead bodies got their attention. That situation probably didn't happen often in Kraken County.

Teresa and Ross were waiting when they roared up to the well. Ross strode forward to meet them, hand extended. "Detective Ross Minatelli, Dallas Police."

The sheriff, an older man with a graying mustache and a slight paunch, accepted his hand. "Richard Laskey, Kraken County Sheriff. This is my deputy, Clint Freemont."

The tall, lanky deputy shook Ross' hand.

Teresa stepped up to join them, stood straight and proud, and held out her hand. "And I'm Teresa Landow, the medium who found this place."

Amanda flinched. Jake had simply told the sheriff they got their information from a "trusted source."

The sheriff stroked his mustache. "Is that right? You're one of those psychics, like on TV?"

"I'm a medium, yes. Detective Minatelli's brother told me his body is in this well."

Ross focused his gaze on a tree off to the side and said nothing.

"Well, then," Laskey said, "let's see what we've got here. We couldn't bring in a lot of fancy equipment, but I think we can handle this."

The four men went to work unloading the small carts. Soon the place was flooded with light and the men were working diligently with ropes and pulleys to raise whatever was in the dark depths of the well.

Amanda would have liked to squeeze in and see what was going on, but she stayed back with Teresa, just outside the lighted area.

"Is Parker here?" she asked quietly.

Teresa nodded. "He's staying close to Ross. He says they're hauling up his body and he knows Ross is going to be upset."

"Does it bother him, seeing his body?"

"No. He's just worried about his brother."

"Didn't bother me," Charley said, "even though there was a big hole in my chest. But it's like it wasn't my chest. I mean, my chest is right here."

"Yeah, Parker says that's what it's like. Omigawd. They're bringing something up."

"Some*thing?*" Amanda gulped. "It's a man. He's wearing blue jeans." That simple item of clothing made the horror worse.

The sheriff and his deputy pulled the body out of the well and rolled it onto the ground.

Teresa clutched Amanda's hand.

For several long moments nobody said a word or moved a muscle.

Ross squatted beside the body.

Jake put a hand on his friend's back.

Ross lifted his head and looked in Teresa's direction. "It's Parker."

Chapter Six

Amanda and Teresa were civilians, Ross was personally involved, and Jake was out of his jurisdiction. They all had to leave while the Kraken County Sheriff's Department came back with more men and more equipment to bring up the other "body or bodies" from the well.

Three people on each four-wheeler was cozy but doable. Amanda didn't mind having Jake's arms wrapped tightly around her, but wrapping hers around Sheriff Laskey's middle was a little weird.

Nevertheless, they made it back and climbed into Ross' car. They sat in darkness and silence watching as Deputy Freemont rode back to the scene and the sheriff's truck drove away to bring more officers.

"You knew." Ross stared out the windshield. "How?"

"I told you." Teresa's words were quiet, little more than a whisper in the night.

"Who did this? Who killed my brother?"

"I don't know that. He won't tell me."

"I see." Ross leaned forward and started the car. They began the journey home through the darkness.

Amanda sat rigidly beside Jake in the back seat. No one spoke, not even Charley.

When they reached the highway, Ross let out a long sigh then cleared his throat. "I can't believe you talked to my brother's spirit."

Teresa turned toward him and opened her mouth to speak.

He held up a hand. "But I don't disbelieve you."

"What the freak does that mean?" Charley demanded.

"What the freak does that mean?" Teresa repeated.

Ross stared straight ahead as the car followed its headlight beams through the night. "I don't know."

"He doesn't know?" Charley asked. "If he doesn't know, then who does?"

No one spoke.

"Go ahead, ask him," Charley said.

Teresa compressed her lips as if holding the words inside. Surely she wasn't going to let Charley goad her into a fight with Ross.

She lifted her chin and looked directly at Ross. "Whether you want to believe or not, your brother has another message for you. Now that you've found his body and know for sure he's dead, he wants you to transfer all his accounts into your name, especially the bank account that his trust fund pays into."

In the rearview mirror Amanda saw the scowl on Ross' face. "At a time like this, you want me to believe my brother's concerned about money?"

Teresa lifted her hands in a defensive gesture. "I'm just repeating the message."

A heavy silence filled the car.

"I could really go for a burger when we get back to civilization," Amanda said. Food was always a good diversion.

"Sounds great to me," Jake said. "I think I saw a Whataburger on the drive down here."

"Whataburger," Amanda repeated. "Great. Yeah. Let's do that. Burger with everything, fries on the side."

"Sounds good to me," Charley said.

No one else commented.

Teresa's cell phone beeped several times. "Guess we're back to civilization. I've got a signal." She took her phone from her purse and studied the display. "That's odd. Nine messages, all from the same number, and it's not a number I recognize."

Jake's cell phone pinged. He took his from his pocket. "I've got eight messages, all from the same number. Teresa, what number called you?"

Teresa read out the digits.

"That's the same person who's been calling me," Jake said.

Amanda studied Jake's phone and repeated the number. "I think that's my sister's number."

Teresa called voice mail and put it on speaker.

"Hi, this is Jenny Carter," said the little-girl voice. "I'm trying to find my sister, Amanda, and she phoned you recently so I thought you might know something. Please return my call as soon as you can."

Amanda groaned. "She found my cell phone. I'm sorry."

"No problem," Teresa assured her. "She's just worried about you."

Another message from Jenny played from her phone, this one a little more frantic.

Jake handed Amanda his cell. "Call her and let her know you're okay."

"Thanks." She took the phone and tapped one of Jenny's calls to return it.

Her sister answered immediately. "Hello?"

"Hi, it's me. I've been with Jake and Teresa all day, and we're heading home now. Sorry you were worried."

"I didn't hear from you and I tried to call you and your phone rang here and I knew you'd left it at home and I couldn't call you and you couldn't call me! Where have you been?"

"It's a long story. I'll tell you when I get home."

"I was just frantic! I called the police—" Amanda cringed— "but they said you had to be missing some really long period of time before they'd investigate and they said I should call your friends, so I did."

"I know. We were out of cell phone range. Sorry."

"I called your assistant and he said you were going out with Jake and Teresa and somebody else on Saturday night, and he hadn't seen you since Saturday noon when the shop closed. He's worried too."

Amanda would have to call Dawson to reassure him she was all right. "Who else did you call?" *Please say no one!*

"I called Charley's mother."

"She called my mother?" Charley exclaimed.

"She seems like a really nice lady," Jenny continued. "She's very worried about you. She said you got into some trouble last spring when you were down there. I didn't know about that. Why didn't you tell me about that?"

"You'd just found out you were pregnant and I didn't want to stress you." Damn! She'd have to call Irene too. She and Herbert would still be up, worrying about her.

"And Sunny Donovan. You never told me about her, either."

Amanda's heart sank to her toes. Sunny was her birth mother, a fact she'd only discovered last spring and had deliberately chosen not to share with her sister.

Sunny would be worried too.

"All right, I'm on my way home. Should be there in half an hour. I need to go so I can call Dawson and Irene and Sunny and tell them I'm okay."

"You don't need to call Sunny. I'll tell her. She's right here."

Chapter Seven

Amanda opened the door of her apartment.

Jenny hurried toward her as fast as her bulk would allow. "We've been so worried!" Her small features were pinched with genuine concern.

"We have." Sunny stood just behind Jenny. "You look exhausted." So did she. Her usual vibrancy didn't quite make it to her eyes or her voice. Even her red hair, so much like Amanda's except for a few strands of white, appeared listless and tired.

Jenny took Amanda's arm and urged her inside. "Where have you been? I've imagined all kinds of horrible things. You always have had a knack for getting into trouble. Remember when you rode off with that guy on a motorcycle and we thought you'd been kidnapped? And the time you were trying to smoke and almost set the house on fire? And—"

"Okay, enough reminiscing about the good old days. I'm sorry."

Jenny frowned, spread a hand on her stomach and rubbed.

Was the baby coming? Amanda looked at Sunny and saw the same panic on her face.

"Are you all right?" Amanda asked.

Jenny sank onto the sofa, still holding her stomach. "Your niece was worried too. She's been kicking like a football player."

"I'm sorry," Amanda repeated. "I went to see Teresa. Ross and Jake came over and we went for a drive in the country."

Jenny and Sunny looked at her expectantly.

"Don't tell her you were out looking for dead bodies," Charley said. "She'll have that baby right here. Then we really won't get any sleep. Babies cry a lot."

"We drove down a long country road and we went for a walk and it just took longer than we thought to get back here. I'm really sorry you all were worried and that you made that drive up here at this time of the night, Sunny."

"Not a problem," Sunny assured her. "I don't have to be in court until tomorrow afternoon. I'm glad your sister called me. I'll sleep better tonight now that I know you're okay." She picked up her purse from beside the sofa. "And speaking of sleep, I'm going to head home and let you all get some."

Jenny struggled to her feet. "I wish we could offer to let you stay here tonight, but Amanda doesn't have a guest room."

"It's okay," Sunny said. "It's only about fifty miles home, and I know a good lawyer who can get me out of a speeding ticket, so I'll make it in half an hour."

"I think that's just wonderful that Amanda has a friend who's a lawyer. Our dad's a judge, and my husband's a lawyer." She frowned at the mention of

Davey. "Can I get you another Coke? Amanda, Sunny doesn't drink coffee either. Amanda is the only one in our family who doesn't. The rest of us love our coffee, but Amanda's never liked it. Very strange that she didn't get the coffee gene. I wonder if my baby will? Davey drinks coffee too."

Sunny grinned and winked at Amanda, sharing the knowledge that she wasn't really the only one in the family who didn't like coffee. Neither did her biological mother.

"A Coke for the road would be great."

Jenny turned and left the room.

"I hope she and her husband patch things up before the baby comes," Sunny said. "I can't picture her as a single mom. She seems kind of...helpless."

Amanda rolled her eyes. "Don't worry about her. She's helpless in a very tough way. She'll be back with her adoring husband long before that baby gets here."

She looked at Jenny's protruding stomach as she waddled back from the kitchen with a red can in each hand. "I hope."

Amanda and Charley walked downstairs with Sunny.

Sunny slid into her little red sports car.

"Text me when you get home safely," Amanda said.

A smile lit Sunny's tired features. "I will. Thanks."

"For what?"

"For caring." She closed the door and roared away.

"If I had the energy," Amanda said, "I'd go back upstairs and kill my sister."

"Not a good idea. What if she comes back as a ghost and you can't get away from her?"

"You're right. Not a good idea."

Amanda climbed the stairs to her apartment.

Jenny sat on the sofa holding a glass of water in one hand, staring at it in disgust. "It seems like a year since I've had a glass of wine or a cup of coffee."

Amanda sank down beside her. "I guess you can't have Coke either?"

Jenny shook her head. "Caffeine."

"Thank God for that," Charley said. "Hyper as she already is, I'd hate to see her after a couple of cups of coffee."

"It won't be long." *Please let it be long enough for her to get back home!*

"Sunny's nice. You met her at Charley's funeral? She knew Charley?"

"She lives in a small town. Everybody knows everybody." Amanda considered leaving it at that, but there was no point in trying to protect Charley's reputation since he had none to start with. "She was Charley's attorney on a drug charge."

"Blabbermouth," Charley said.

"Oh!" Jenny's eyes widened and she lifted a hand to her mouth. "That doesn't surprise me. I never trusted that man."

Charley made a rude noise. "I never trusted you either."

Amanda looked down at her hands. She was not going to laugh at Charley's rude comment. She bit her lip. She absolutely was not going to laugh.

"She looks familiar," Jenny said. "Have I met her before?"

"Who?"

"Sunny."

Charley burst into eerie laughter. "Duh! She looks like you. Or you look like her. How dense can your sister be?"

Charley wasn't funny anymore.

"Wouldn't it be hilarious," he continued, "if she figured out who Sunny is and realized dear old Dad isn't a saint and your mother..." His voice trailed off. "Or maybe it wouldn't be hilarious."

It would definitely not be hilarious. On a good day, Jenny would have major hysterics should she learn the distressing and scandalous truth about her family. And this was far from a good day. When the story of Amanda's birth came out a few months before, they had all agreed that Jenny did not need to know. *She's too delicate*, her mother said. *She's too ditzy,* their father said. As usual, Amanda agreed with her father.

"Sunny's a lawyer," Amanda said. "You probably saw her at one of the parties Davey dragged you to or one of the dinners Mother had for Dad's associates."

Jenny's forehead creased, but she nodded. "I guess." She yawned and ran a hand through her short, dark hair. "Well, I'm exhausted. Past my bedtime."

"Guess that means she's going to sleep here again tonight," Charley grumbled.

"So," Amanda said, "did you talk to Davey today?" She tried not to look too eager.

Jenny shifted her shoulders in a casual shrug. "He called, but I didn't answer. He called your number too. I didn't answer that either."

"You can't work things out if you don't talk to him."

"I don't want to work things out. My mind is made up." She leaned over and kissed Amanda's cheek. "I'm glad you're home safe." She struggled to her feet and staggered to the bedroom.

Damn. That last comment and gesture took a lot of the steam out of Amanda's anger at her sister.

Dawson was hard at work repairing the shovel head engine of a 1971 Harley Davidson FX Super Glide when Amanda got down to the shop the next morning.

"Sorry I'm late." She made her way to the small office at the back of the work room to get a Coke. She'd dressed as quickly and quietly as possible to avoid waking Jenny and hadn't wanted to risk opening the refrigerator and popping the top on a can of Coke.

Dawson looked up over the frames of his glasses as she walked by and gave her his shy smile. "I think it's okay if you're late since you're the boss. Everything all right with your sister?"

"She's still asleep. Sorry about the hassle yesterday." Amanda reached the back room, retrieved a Coke from the small refrigerator and took a long, slow, delicious gulp.

"No problem," Dawson called. "I wasn't worried. You can take care of yourself. I've seen you do it."

Amanda sat down at the cluttered desk and took her cell phone from her pocket. Such a small object to have caused so much trouble yesterday.

She looked at her list of missed calls. As Jenny had said, Davey had phoned yesterday and left a voice mail.

"Amanda, this is David Carter, Jenny's husband." Duh. "I'm very worried about her and the baby. She's been gone for two days. If you hear from her, would you please let me know?"

Returning his call would be the polite thing to do. It wasn't as if she was interfering in her sister's affairs. He'd called her first.

He answered immediately.

"Hi, Davey. This is Amanda. I've got your wife."

"Is she okay? Is the baby okay?"

"Jenny and the baby are fine. I think she'd like to come home—"

Charley burst into laughter. "You'd like her to go home."

"But you know how stubborn she can be," Amanda continued. "I don't know what you all fought about, but I'm sure if you were to show up with roses or a box of chocolates—"

"She can't eat chocolate with the baby."

71

"Remind me never to get pregnant," Amanda mumbled.

"What?"

"I'm sure the baby will have no objection to roses. Or a piece of jewelry." Surely there was a piece of jewelry out there somewhere that Jenny didn't have. "Mostly I think she'd just like to know you're concerned. Come by and tell her you're sorry about whatever happened."

"But I don't know what happened. I came home to find her gone and a note saying she couldn't take it anymore. She didn't say what it was she can't take anymore. She's been a little temperamental since she got pregnant."

And before she got pregnant. Amanda took another long drink of her soda. "It doesn't matter what she can't take anymore. Yes, she's a little irrational right now. Hormones and all. Just bring her flowers and jewelry and tell her you're sorry."

"How can I apologize when I don't know what I did wrong?"

Amanda looked toward the ceiling. Instead of divine guidance, she saw only Charley.

"It's easy. Open your mouth and say, *Jenny, I'm sorry, I miss you, I love you, please come home.*"

Silence.

"Pretend you're trying to convince a client to sign a contract."

"There's a diamond and emerald ring she's been wanting."

"Good! Get her that and say the words I taught you. *Jenny, I'm sorry, I miss you, I love you, please come home.*"

"I'll have to get a larger size since her fingers are swollen from the pregnancy. She could have it resized after the baby comes."

"Bad idea. Get her a necklace. Her neck isn't swollen. What did I tell you to say?"

"Jenny, I'm sorry, I miss you, I love you, please come home."

"Perfect. I've got to go. A customer just came in."

"Thank you, Amanda."

She disconnected the call. "If I had to talk to him every day, I'd be as nuts as my sister."

"He has to talk to your sister," Charley said. "That would make anybody crazy."

"I'm going to work on a nice, uncomplicated motorcycle."

"I'll help."

"In that case, I need another Coke."

She tucked her phone into her back pocket to keep it close. The list of people who might call was getting longer by the minute. Davey, Jenny, Jake, Teresa, Ross—and she didn't expect good news from any of them.

❧

Amanda, Dawson, and Jenny were finishing the salads Jenny had delivered for their lunch when Teresa burst into the shop.

"Amanda!"

"Back here in the office."

Teresa paused in the doorway, her gaze wild as it darted back and forth at the three of them. "I need...is there somewhere we can talk in private?"

"I'm done." Dawson rose and picked up his almost empty plastic container. "I have an engine to work on."

Jenny rose also. "I don't think we've met. I'm Jenny Carter, Amanda's sister." She extended a hand.

Teresa's expression became even wilder as she accepted Jenny's hand. "Nice to meet you. I'm Teresa Landow."

"Oh, you're Teresa! You and Amanda had quite the adventure yesterday. I'm so glad you're both okay. Sunny and I were quite worried. Do you know Sunny? She's a friend of Amanda's. She met him at Charley's funeral."

Teresa gave Amanda a desperate look.

Charley twirled a finger around his ear to indicate Jenny was nuts.

"No, Teresa hasn't met Sunny." Amanda lifted the container holding the rest of Jenny's salad. "Why don't you take this upstairs and eat in a cleaner place where you don't have to smell paint and grease?"

"Oh! Of course. I understand. You want to talk in private. I'll just go upstairs and leave the two of you alone." She crossed the room then turned back at the door. "Nice to meet you, Teresa. I'm staying with Amanda for a while. My husband and I are separated, and I'm pregnant. I'm so grateful to Amanda for taking me in." She wiggled her fingers in a cutesy good-bye and left, closing the door behind her.

Teresa sank into the folding chair and pressed her hands to the side of her face. "You're not going to believe. I don't know where to start."

"How about the middle?" Amanda sat in the chair behind the desk.

Teresa spread her hands and drew in a deep breath. "Ross is rich."

Chapter Eight

"Ross is..." Amanda repeated. "What?"

"Well, you did tell her to start in the middle," Charley said.

"I'm pretty sure Dallas doesn't pay cops exorbitant salaries. How did Ross get rich? Did he take bribes or inherit the family fortune?"

"Actually," Teresa said, "he did. Inherit the family fortune, not take bribes."

Amanda went to the small refrigerator, retrieved two Cokes, and handed one to Teresa.

"We may need something stronger than Coke for this," Teresa said. "Have you got a bottle of wine tucked away in that little refrigerator? Better yet, a bottle of tequila?"

Amanda popped the top of her can. "No, I think I need to be completely sober for this." She sat down and took a long drink then leaned back in the office chair and put her feet on the desk. "Okay, Ross is rich."

"He told me about it last night. We had a long talk." She smiled and a faint glow suffused her cheeks. "He still can't totally accept the spirit thing, but he said he cares for me. He wants us to be exclusive. I thought we already were, but it was nice to hear him put it into words, and it was really cute to see Mr. Macho Cop blush and stammer."

Teresa seemed more interested in the caring part, not the rich part. Interesting. "Okay, he wants you to have an exclusive relationship. That's good. How about the rich part? His family's wealthy? Didn't he say his parents were dead?"

"Yes, they are. His dad was a cop who got killed on the job when Ross was three."

"Another cop? So where does the money come in?"

"Probably stole it from a drug bust," Charley said.

Teresa's lips thinned. "Really, Charley?"

He shrugged and looked away. "I guess not."

Teresa turned her attention back to Amanda. "Two years after Ross' father died, his mother married Nicholas Minatelli who adopted Ross and raised him. He barely remembers his real father except what his mother told him, but it was enough to make him decide to be a cop."

"So his step father wasn't a cop?"

"No, he came over from Italy and opened a small pizza parlor. He was making enough money to pay the bills and was perfectly happy with that, but Ross' mother saw potential. She jumped in and helped him turn it into a chain which they sold for a lot of money when Ross was twenty-five. But they didn't get to enjoy their wealth for long. They were in Hawaii on vacation, took one of those helicopter tours and crashed."

Amanda flinched. "That's horrible!"

"Yeah. Ross doesn't like to talk about it. That's why he hadn't said anything before. All the money went into trust funds for him and Parker. He hasn't touched his. He associates the money with the death of his parents."

"And Parker is Ross' half-brother?"

Teresa nodded. "Technically, yes, but Parker came along a couple of years after Ross' mom married his step dad, so they grew up together. Parker is his little brother, and he's always taken care of him. Parker was only seventeen when his parents were killed, so he got an allowance from his trust until he turned twenty-one, which was last year. A few months ago he changed, became very secretive, something he'd never been before." She stopped talking and looked around the room.

Amanda and Charley followed her gaze.

"It's okay," Teresa said. "I just wanted to be sure he isn't here. It feels weird talking about him in front of him. He was with me most of the night. After Ross left, he confirmed everything Ross said, that they were close and Ross took care of him after their parents died. Then he had charge of his own money and his own life. Suddenly it hit him that his parents were really gone and he had to become an adult. He won't tell me what he was being secretive about, but he didn't deny there was something he doesn't want to talk about. He just said it wasn't important."

"Good grief," Amanda said. "There sure are a lot of things that aren't important to dead people."

"Hey!" Charley protested. "Don't stereotype dead people. Lots of things are important to me."

Like seeing to it that she and Jake didn't spend time alone together.

"What was important to him," Amanda said, "was that Ross find his body and get his accounts transferred into Ross' name?"

Teresa nodded. "Ross was designated the beneficiary of the trust if anything happened to Parker."

"But what difference would it make if Ross is already rich? Not like he's going to lose his house if he doesn't get his brother's money now instead of seven years from now if he had to wait to have him declared legally dead. And if that was the reason, why is he still here since he's already done that?"

"I'll ask him next time he comes around, but I doubt if he'll tell me." Teresa looked at Charley. "Why did you come back to Amanda?"

"I came back to save her from Kimball, the man who murdered me."

Amanda leveled her gaze at him. "And Kimball is now in prison serving life without parole. Why are you still here?"

Charley considered her question for a moment. Finally he looked down at the floor. "I don't know. So maybe Parker doesn't know either."

No one spoke for a long moment.

"I think he knows," Teresa finally said. "He seems determined and purposeful. Maybe it's something as simple as not wanting Ross to worry about him. But I don't understand why he doesn't just tell me that."

"I don't understand why he doesn't tell you who killed him," Charley said. "I told Amanda right away. They tried to blame her for killing me."

"Because I had plenty of motive. Are they trying to blame you for Parker's death, Teresa?"

Teresa leaned back in the metal chair. "I told Sheriff Laskey last night that Ross' brother led us to the bodies through me. He didn't say anything at the time, but now he wants me to come in and explain how I knew where to find a well full of bodies. That's what I get for being honest."

"It would have come up eventually. Jake told him we got the information from a trusted source. He'd have wanted to know the name of that trusted source, and you know neither of them would ever lie to another officer of the law." Amanda was learning that the occasional white lie could serve a good purpose, but Jake and Ross were the ultimate cops. "So when do you have to go in?"

"Next couple of days. He was nice about it, but he seems to think I can tell him something that will help solve the case. I can't because Parker won't tell me."

Amanda nodded slowly. "I see. You've got to convince the sheriff that you knew where to find the bodies because you talked to one of the dead men who told you where his body was but he won't tell you who murdered him. Maybe you need a lawyer."

"People always get lawyers on TV." Since Charley could no longer go to bars, scam people, pick up women and gamble, he spent a lot of time watching TV.

"Yeah, I need somebody who's tough and who won't think I'm nuts because I talk to dead people."

"Actually, I may know somebody like that." Sunny was smart, tough, and if she accepted that Amanda saw Charley, surely she'd accept that Teresa communed with other spirits. "I'll call her."

"Thanks." Teresa turned to Charley. "Yesterday when we were walking through the woods, what were you and Parker talking about when you went off to the side together?"

Charley shrugged in an apparent attempt to look casual, but his expression was pleased. "Spiritual stuff. He's new to this whole ghost thing and he needs guidance."

Amanda shuddered. "Please don't guide him."

"That was very nice of you," Teresa said. "You can be a big help to him. Did you discuss how it felt to leave your bodies?"

Charley nodded. "We were both confused at first. He's still a little confused, but he's getting better."

"Did you talk about how it felt to be murdered?"

"We didn't get that far. It was mostly how to move around from place to place and how to control coming back to visit with you all."

"Next time we see him, could you ask him who killed him? Maybe he'll tell you. I'd kind of like to know so I can stay out of jail."

"Oh!" Charley grinned. "I can do that. Yeah, he'll tell me. We have a bond."

"I would really appreciate that, Charley." Teresa rose. "All right, I'll let you get back to work."

The two women and one ghost strolled through the shop to the front door.

"Good to see you, Dawson," Teresa said.

Dawson looked up from his work. "Good to see you, Teresa."

Amanda closed the door behind her friend and started back across the shop.

"I like her." Dawson didn't look up.

"Yes," Amanda said. "I do too."

"I hope everything works out about finding the dead guys."

Amanda stopped in the middle of the floor. "Did you overhear us talking?"

"No. I see things on the Internet."

"What did you see?"

"That she led authorities to a well with twenty bodies in it, and she said their spirits took her there."

"It was only five bodies and one spirit."

"Oh, good." He dismissed the subject and continued with his work, putting an engine back together.

Charley lifted his eyebrows. "What's wrong with him? That's not good at all."

Dawson looked up again. "Parker Minatelli was related to Ross, right? It's not a common last name. Did Ross know any of the other people? Did he know Steven Anderson?"

"Who? I don't know. Who's Steven Anderson?"

"The only body besides Parker that they've identified so far. He's why it's all over the Internet. He's Senator Glen Anderson's son."

Chapter Nine

Amanda raced out the door, trying to catch Teresa. It was too late. The little blue convertible flew down the street as if determined to catch a speeding ticket.

She turned to Charley. "Stop her! She needs to ask Parker about Steven Anderson."

Charley dashed after the car but returned almost immediately, a sullen look on his face. "I got to the end of my leash and you yanked me back."

"I'm not any happier about this attachment to me than you are." Amanda took her cell phone from her pocket and punched in Teresa's number. She got voice mail. Of course Teresa couldn't hear her phone ringing over the sound of the wind rushing past her at eighty miles an hour. "This is Amanda. One of the bodies has been identified. Steven Anderson. Ask Parker if he knows him. Knew him. Whatever. Call me."

"Amanda?"

She whirled around at the sound of her name. "Davey?"

"Sorry. I didn't mean to startle you." Her sister's husband blinked in the sunlight and smiled apologetically. In his dark gray suit, white shirt and blue tie, he looked every inch the tax lawyer he was. But for the first time since she'd known him, the man looked slightly rumpled. Only slightly. Considering he was wearing a suit in the Texas sun and his pregnant wife had left him, he remained remarkably cool.

Amanda shoved her phone into her back pocket. "It's okay. I was just—uh—a friend left and I was trying to catch her."

"The brunette in the BMW?"

"Yeah, that's the one. Have you talked to Jenny yet?"

"I knocked on the door, but she's not there. I came down when I saw you out here. Do you know where she's gone?"

Amanda pointed toward the white Mercedes parked a few feet away. "She's here. Maybe she's sleeping."

Davey shook his head. "That's not her car. That's mine."

"Matching Mercedes," Charley said. "Isn't that just adorable?"

"She was here a few minutes ago," Amanda said. "We had lunch together. Maybe she decided to go home."

He looked down at the pavement. "I doubt it." He lifted his gaze. "Would you tell her I was here? And give her this?" He held out a small gift box wrapped in silver paper with a pink bow.

She accepted the box and looked it over. "Pink for the baby?"

He nodded.

"I hope this gift has nothing to do with the baby. She needs something that's just for her." She shook the box and heard faint movement. "This better not be a rattle."

"It's a diamond necklace, just like we talked about."

"She can add it to her collection," Charley said. "Pretty soon she'll be renting a storage unit for her diamonds. Or does she already have one?"

Amanda refused to look at Charley. She might laugh if she did. "Good choice."

"Diamonds are her birthstone."

"I'll bet her mother timed it that way on purpose," Charley said.

She handed the box back to Davey. "You better keep this. It will mean so much more coming directly from you. And maybe she's already gone home."

He accepted the box. "That would be wonderful if I return to find her there. Thank you, Amanda, for taking care of my Jenny. This pregnancy has been hard on her. She's so delicate."

"No problem," Amanda assured him. "It's a chance for us to share this special time together."

Charley burst into laughter, pounding the air with one fist. "You're a lousy actress. That came out sounding totally phony."

Davey smiled. For a moment she thought he was going to hug her. Davey was not the affectionate type. Amanda liked that about him. He nodded and turned to go then stopped. "Did I hear you say something about Steven Anderson? Would that be Senator Anderson's son?"

"Don't tell him anything," Charley said.

Amanda thought about Charley's warning but couldn't see any reason not to tell Davey something he'd soon see on the news. "They found his body in an old well. Homicide."

Davey sighed. "I'm sorry to hear that but not surprised. How long has he been dead?"

"I haven't heard. Did you know him?"

Davey nodded. "The senator and your dad are friends. Jenny and I hosted a couple of dinners during his campaign. He's a good man, and he's been very worried about his son. I hate to hear he's dead, but at least Glen will have some closure now."

"*Closure*?" Charley mimicked. "He doesn't know much about death if he thinks it's some kind of closure."

"What happened? Was Steven kidnapped or something?"

Davey shook his head. "He got in with the wrong crowd. He was taking drugs and got arrested twice over the last couple of years. Those are the only times Glen heard from him, when he needed bail money. Very sad when you hope your son gets arrested just so you can hear from him and know he's okay."

"Drugs," Charley said. "There's your connection to Parker. He got a lot of money and got all secretive. He was probably using and—"

"That is sad," Amanda said. She didn't want to think that Ross' little brother had been on drugs. Besides, he'd have told Teresa if he was. Wouldn't he? However, he was keeping a lot of things secret, a lot of things he didn't consider *important*. "So Steven's father hasn't heard from him in a while?"

"A few months. I'm not sure exactly how long. I'll have to express my condolences. Jenny will want to..." He stopped and swallowed.

"Yes," Amanda assured him, "she will want to send flowers and visit with the family and do all the right things. If I see her before you do, I'll tell her."

"Thank you." Again Davey looked as if he might want to hug Amanda. Instead he extended a hand.

Amanda took his hand, pulled him to her and gave him a quick hug along with a pat on the back. "It's going to be fine."

He left, driving away in the white car that matched his wife's.

"You think they have matching underwear?" Charley asked.

It was entirely possible. "Shut up." Amanda turned and started up the steps to her apartment.

"Better check and be sure your sister didn't run away with your store brand soap and shampoo." He laughed again.

Had she really once thought he had a nice laugh? Had she really once thought he was a nice man?

"I want to see if her luggage is still there or if she went home."

"She wouldn't go home without telling you. That would be rude. Her mother would never tolerate such behavior."

"She came over here without telling me." Amanda strode into her apartment and straight to the bedroom. Jenny's suitcases sat open on the floor, various garments spilling out.

"Told you she wouldn't leave." He darted through the wall. "Here's a note in the kitchen. She says she's gone shopping and will be back in time for dinner."

Amanda picked up a filmy white garment from the floor and put it on top of the clothes in the suitcase. "Oh, goody. I was afraid we'd have to eat alone again."

Charley appeared beside her. "You were?"

"No."

Her phone rang. She pulled it from her pocket. Teresa.

"I just got home," she said. "I didn't want to answer my phone while I was driving. Tell me about Steven Anderson. How did you find out he was one of the victims?"

"Dawson saw it on the Internet. I just learned he's been involved in the drug scene. Any chance Parker was doing drugs and met Anderson in that world?"

"Parker, were you using drugs? Did you know Steven Anderson?" A pause. "He says he wasn't using drugs and he didn't know the man."

"Too bad. That might have given us a clue as to who killed him."

"Gotta go," Teresa said. "Ross is calling. Bye."

Charley looked at the phone and snorted. "That was rude."

Amanda shoved her phone into her back pocket. "No, it wasn't. She got another call. We didn't have anything else to say and I've got to get back to work. One of us has to make the money to pay the bills so you can watch television all night."

"Can't watch it while you're sleeping in the living room," he grumbled, following her out of the apartment. "Maybe your sister's shopping for a guest room for you."

It was always possible.

Amanda made it inside the door of her shop before her phone rang again.

"You're never going to believe what just happened," Teresa said.

"Let me see...you sound ecstatic after talking to Ross. He proposed?"

Dawson looked up from his work and smiled. Amanda returned the smile and continued toward the office at the back.

"No—"

Charley hovered close to the phone. "He told you your ex was killed in a prison fight by somebody named Shankie?"

"No! Charley, be quiet a minute," Teresa said. "This is important. Ross went to the bank today to transfer that account his brother mentioned, and he found out some woman named Lila Stone has been getting automated payments from it."

"Parker, you dog!" Charley grinned. "Got you a—"

"A girl friend?" Amanda interrupted.

"We don't know what her relationship to him is. But the good news is, Ross called me and requested I ask Parker who she is."

"That's great. You've made a believer out of him."

"Sort of. He started the conversation with, *Not that I really believe you can talk to my brother, but if you can...*"

"Okay, that's progress. So what did Parker say when you asked him?"

Teresa sighed. "What do you think? He said it's not important."

Amanda sank into the chair behind her desk, put her chin in her free hand and groaned. "Of course. What did Ross say when you told him that?"

"It didn't make him happy."

"Maybe," Charley said, "Parker doesn't think you and Ross should be together, so he's deliberately sabotaging your relationship. Maybe..."

"Shut up," Amanda said.

"I haven't got to the best part yet," Teresa said. "With Steven Anderson being the son of a senator, the whole state is getting involved in the investigation. No way Ross can get into Parker's apartment until they finish searching it, and who knows if there'll even be anything left to find when they get through with it? So he can't look for information about this Lila Stone, and if the cops find her name, they'll be hot on her tracks. He's taken a leave of absence and he wants to go question her before anybody else gets to her."

"Makes sense."

"And he wants me to go with him and bring Parker so I can relay his questions and see how Parker reacts."

"I can see how questioning Parker's former girlfriend or whatever she is while dragging along his ghost could be a bonding moment for you and Ross."

"I think it will be. This will be the time he finally accepts my talent."

Teresa had taken Amanda's sarcastic comment seriously. "Well, let me know how it goes." *And good luck with that.*

"Actually, I'd like for you to be there. I need you to bring Charley since he seems to have established a relationship with Parker."

"Bring Charley?" Amanda did not want to get involved in a situation that promised to have no good outcome. "Why don't you just do whatever it is you do to make him go with you? I don't have to be there."

"Okay, thanks, I'll do that."

"Hey!" Charley protested. "I'm right here! I can hear you! Anybody think about asking me if I want to go?"

Amanda twisted around and arched an eyebrow. "Like you have a choice?"

"I'm sorry, Charley," Teresa said. "I apologize for leaving you out. Would you please come with me to question Parker's girl friend? Maybe you can even get him to tell us who murdered him."

"Well..."

"I'll get you a margarita next time we go out for Mexican food."

"Just you, me and Amanda? No guys?"

Amanda wasn't sure what teeth gnashing sounded like, but she felt certain Teresa was doing it during the long moment of silence that followed Charley's request.

"Yes," Teresa agreed. "The three of us will go out for Mexican food without the guys if you'll help me. Deal?"

Charley stood back, pressed his hands together and halfway through each other and looked thoughtful. "I think Parker will tell me more than he tells you since he and I have a lot in common, both of us being spiritual. He's an all right guy. I like him better than his brother."

That wasn't surprising. Parker was dead so he wasn't a serious rival for Teresa's attention. Would Charley change his mind if Teresa spent too much time with Parker during the planned interview?

"Great!" Teresa said. "Thank you."

"Wait a minute," Charley protested. "We haven't finished working out the terms of our deal."

"We haven't? I thought the evening out was your payment."

"It's part of it. There's one more term. Amanda comes with us."

"Okay. Amanda comes with us."

"Wait a minute," Amanda protested. "To quote someone we heard from recently, 'Anybody think about asking me if I want to go?' The answer is, no. I don't want to go."

Charley fisted his hands on his hips defiantly. "If you don't go, I don't go."

"You have to go if Teresa does whatever it is she does and takes you."

"Maybe I have to go, but I don't have to talk when I get there. I'm not talking to Parker unless you're there."

"Why not?" Charley liked Teresa and had gone with her before. It was the only way Amanda had been able to be alone with Jake. And that was it, of course. "Oh, I get it. You want to be sure I can't see Jake while you're gone. How about I give you my word?"

Charley shook his head. "Not good enough. You could lie. I can't, but you can. I've heard you."

"Charley, I really don't want to go along on this expedition. How's Teresa going to explain my presence? *Amanda came along because she has her own personal ghost and he can talk to my ghost?* Really?"

Charley lifted his chin. "Really."

"Please, Amanda," Teresa entreated. "I want this to go well, and I'm concerned that Parker won't tell me what I need to know. If I can't answer the questions Ross asks, he's going to think I'm a fraud. I really need Charley's help communicating with him."

Amanda opened her mouth to refuse again but couldn't do it. Teresa had said *please*. Teresa sounded desperate. Teresa needed her help. Teresa was her friend. She sighed. "All right, fine, I'll go."

"Thank you, thank you! Ross wants to talk to this Lila person before the cops find her, before she becomes a person of interest because then he won't be able to talk to her since he's not officially on the case. He's on his way now. Can you bring Charley and come on over?"

No wonder Amanda had never before had a best friend. They could be a lot of hassle.

Chapter Ten

Teresa and Ross were waiting when Amanda rode up on her bike.

Ross got out of his car and opened the back passenger door. "Thanks for coming along, Amanda." He wasn't smiling. He didn't look thrilled to see her.

"Yeah, sure, no problem. Glad I could help." She pulled off her helmet, climbed into the back seat and set it down beside her. Ross closed the door behind her and got into the driver's seat. What reason had Teresa given him for her presence?

From the passenger seat, Teresa turned to face her. "Yes, thank you so much for coming. I explained to Ross how talking to spirits sometimes saps my energy, and it really helps to have a person around who exudes high energy like you do."

Charley laughed. "I think she just called you hyper."

Amanda bared her teeth in a phony smile. Ross' attention was focused on driving out of the parking lot so only Teresa saw it. "Give me another Coke or two, and I'll exude off the walls for you." She looked around the car. "Is he here now?"

"No," Teresa and Charley both said at the same time.

"He's not happy about this visit to Lila Stone," Teresa said.

He'd been paying the woman money. Surely that meant he liked her and might even enjoy seeing her again. "Why not?"

Teresa rolled her eyes. "Same old thing. It's not important."

"It's almost twenty thousand dollars of importance," Ross said.

"He finally agreed to meet us there when we— Ross—pointed out that with half the law enforcement in the state looking into this case, they're going to find her eventually. Talking to us first will prepare her for that interrogation. So Parker agreed to meet us. He wants to help her."

"Does she know he's...uh..."

"Dead?" Charley finished for her. "You can't say the word? You have no trouble using that word to me, telling me our wedding vows don't count anymore because I'm that word."

"She heard about Parker's death on the news," Teresa said.

"And she's okay with us coming to talk to her about him?" Amanda asked.

"She was a little reluctant at first."

"She was a lot reluctant at first." Ross stared straight ahead as he spoke. "She said she was grieving and didn't want to talk to anybody. I appealed to her as Parker's brother. I told her if I'd found out about her relationship with Parker, the sheriff would find out also so maybe we should talk about it first. Get her prepared for dealing with the sheriff."

"I see," Amanda said. "Where does she live? Where are we going?"

"South of town. South of Duncanville, actually."

"So she's sort of on the way to the place where we found Parker's body? That's a coincidence."

"Are we going back to that place?" Charley complained. "I changed my mind about going with you if that's where we're headed. I didn't like that place."

Teresa turned to him and lowered her brows.

"Yes, it's a coincidence," Ross said. "But it's nothing definitive. A lot of people live down that way. I just want to talk to her in an unofficial capacity, find out what her relationship with my brother was. Anything I find out that relates to solving the case, of course I'll turn it over to the proper authorities."

"Of course," Teresa repeated.

"Of course," Amanda said.

Charley laughed.

They rode in silence for a few minutes.

"Maybe she killed him," Charley said. He never had been good at the quiet game. "I don't want to talk to a murderess. What if she tries to kill us? Amanda, did you bring your Smith and Wesson?"

Lila Stone would have a tough time killing Charley. If it was that easy, Amanda would have done it herself when he first came back into her life after he died.

"We need to ask Parker," Charley continued. "Why isn't he here? Why is he meeting us there? Does he just go wherever he wants? I guess some ghosts aren't on a leash. Must be nice."

What if Parker didn't show up? What would Ross think of Teresa's ability then? He'd probably think she'd been lying the whole time. This visit had the potential to be a total disaster. Charley wasn't the only one who didn't want to go.

They drove a few more miles down the highway then exited onto a side road where the residences were farther apart and individual mailboxes sat at the end of gravel driveways. Ross turned down one of the driveways. A brown mobile home squatted in the middle of a desolate but tidy yard. A mid-size white sedan sat under a carport on one side of the house. No old cars, no tractor parts like the yards of some of the neighbors. A couple of gnarled mesquite trees near the house provided neither shade nor the feeling of serenity that came from Amanda's big live oak in her parking lot next to her apartment. Tufts of grass dotted the barren ground. In spite of the row of bright yellow chrysanthemums blooming in front of the house, it felt lonely and sad.

"This place is creepy," Charley said.

"How old is this woman?" Amanda asked. "This doesn't look like someplace a young person lives."

"Twenty-six." Ross put the car in park and got out.

"Ross knows all about her. He ran a complete background check on her," Teresa said. "She dropped out of high school in her junior year. Been picked up a couple of times for drugs and once for prostitution. Her mother died a year ago and left this place to her."

There was the drug thing again. Drug usage had become a big problem everywhere so it could be just a coincidence.

Or not.

The screen door of the house opened. A short, slim woman with medium length blond hair stepped onto the porch. In her faded jeans—probably a size zero—and her white blouse with ruffles down the front and on the sleeves, she could have been a child until Amanda got close enough to see her face. She looked older than twenty-six years. Tiny wrinkles creased her eyes and upper lip. Her nose and chin pinched into sharp edges.

"That woman's using," Charley said.

And Charley would know. He'd been involved with drugs and drug users more than a few times.

"Lila?" Ross paused at the edge of the porch. "I'm Ross Minatelli, Parker's brother. I spoke to you on the phone."

"Yeah, I'm Lila Stone. Who are these people? I thought you were coming alone." Her wary gaze darted from Ross to Amanda to Teresa.

Ross introduced them. "Teresa and Amanda were with me when we found Parker. They wanted to come today to offer their condolences."

Lila regarded the three of them for a moment then finally shrugged, stepped back and held the door open, inviting them in.

They walked into the smell of stale cigarette smoke and some kind of overpowering floral air freshener. That would explain Lila's wrinkles. Well, the cigarette smoke would, not necessarily the air freshener, though at that potency, it couldn't be ruled out.

"Y'all have a seat," she invited. "I'll get some iced tea." She spoke the conventional words of hospitality but her tone was wooden.

Grief over Parker's death? Distress at having two strange women suddenly appear at her door? Drugs?

The three of them sank onto the sofa, huddling together in a group, leaving the matching chair for Lila.

"I'm going to make sure she doesn't put anything in that tea." Charley followed her to the kitchen.

He was being melodramatic.

Amanda hoped he was.

She looked around the room. Off-white paint covered the living room walls in a pristine way that appeared to be fresh. The brown leather sofa and glass-topped coffee table with a bowl of colorful balls looked new. The pictures on the wall, the two matching lamps sitting on matching tables, the vase on an occasional table...everything was perfect, as if it had come straight off a furniture showroom floor— no personal touches. The neat, tidy interior of the house felt as barren as the outside.

Amanda bit her lip and tried not to be judgmental. Just because her own furnishings ran to mismatched, eclectic pieces didn't mean other people had that same taste.

Lila came back into the room with four matching glasses of iced tea. Again with the matching.

"Nice place," Amanda said. Perhaps her kind words would make up for her tacky thoughts.

"Thank you." Lila handed out the glasses then sat in the arm chair and sipped from her own drink. "I grew up in this house. After Mama died, I tried to spiffy it up a little."

"Very nice." Teresa sounded as phony as Amanda felt. She nudged Amanda's arm and nodded toward the flat screen television in the corner of the room.

"Parker!" Charley darted in that direction. "I was worried you wouldn't come."

Well, the gang's all here. The party can begin. Amanda took a drink of her iced tea since Charley hadn't reported that Lila put any drugs or poison in the beverage.

It was freshly brewed, a little weak but better than some.

"Thank you for letting us come by," Ross said.

Lila grimaced or smiled. It was hard to tell the difference on her harsh features. "Parker told me about you. He said you're a good guy even if you are a cop."

Ross laughed, the sound easy and natural...and probably rehearsed. He was moving into the cop mode thing. "I'm not here as a cop. I'm here as Parker's brother. I took a leave of absence after his death. I just wanted to talk to you because you were important to him."

Lila's eyebrows lifted slightly as if in surprise. "He told you about me?"

Ross nodded. "Of course he did."

Unlike ghosts, cops could lie. However, it was kind of the truth since Parker's bank account had led Ross to this woman, so he'd sort of told Ross about her.

"He told me too," Teresa said. "He told me you're a friend, someone he cares about."

"He did," Charley assured Amanda. "Just now. I heard him."

Lila set her glass of tea precisely in the center of a coaster on the lamp table beside her chair and looked down at the beige carpet...the new, spotless beige carpet. "Parker was a good person."

"Yes." Ross leaned closer, his gaze intent, scrutinizing Lila's every movement—a human lie detector. "He was a very good person. He wanted to help you."

Lila put her face in her hands. Her small shoulders heaved and she burst into sobs.

Charley spread his hands in a gesture of confusion. "Why is she pretending to cry? How does Ross know Parker wanted to help her? He didn't say that. Just because he was giving her money doesn't mean he wanted to help her. She could have been blackmailing him. I'm not buying this boo-hoo stuff."

The same thought had crossed Amanda's mind. Crossed it and lingered. Parker probably had a good reason for wanting to help Lila, but the woman reminded Amanda of a possum with her pointy little face and beady eyes, a possum sneaking around in the dark, getting into garbage cans in somebody's back yard and making a huge mess of things.

Charley looked at the television. "Was she blackmailing you, buddy?" He returned his attention to Amanda. "He says no. But he may be able to lie. I don't trust this Lila."

Charley was cynical, judged others by his own deplorable ethics. Lila had done nothing to justify such an attitude. Nevertheless, Amanda was inclined to agree.

Ross crossed the room to stand beside Lila. He laid a gentle hand on her back. "My brother wanted to save the world. He brought home stray dogs and cats and once even a wounded skunk."

Was he implying Parker had rescued her? From what?

Lila lifted her head. Tears streaked the harsh planes of her face. She really was crying. "I can see him doing that." She took a package of cigarettes and a lighter from behind the lamp then lit up, inhaling deeply before blowing the smoke into the room.

Charley waved a hand in front of his face as if the smoke offended him. "I never did like women who smoked."

Maybe he hadn't liked them, but he'd certainly partied with a lot of them. The cigarette smoke association might explain some of Amanda's instant dislike for this woman. She should give her a chance before judging her.

Lila looked at the cigarette as if surprised to see it in her hand then crushed it out in a glass ashtray next to the lamp. "I'm sorry. Nasty habit. I'm trying to quit."

The one puff seemed to have calmed her and she managed a weak smile. "I miss him. He was a great guy. I loved him."

Amanda sucked in a breath. She'd never known Parker, but she couldn't imagine Ross' brother being with this woman in a loving relationship. Much easier to believe she'd been blackmailing him.

Charley made a face. "She's a skank, Parker. You could have done better."

"Were you lovers?" Teresa asked the question of the blank television screen.

Teresa was talking to Parker, but Lila's eyes widened in horror. She shook her head adamantly. "No! No, he was my...friend. We never...no!"

Parker was...had been...single. Lila was single. There was no reason they shouldn't have been lovers. Whether they were or weren't seemed more inconsequential than Lila's vehement denial warranted.

Frustration spread over Teresa's features. She stood and moved closer to the television. "You were just friends?"

Lila scowled. "Are you talking to me or the television?"

Teresa turned to face her and gave her best phony smile. "You, of course."

Lila's lips thinned and her eyes narrowed. "I thought you said he told you about me."

Teresa bit her lip. Busted.

A thick silence filled the room.

"He did tell us." Amanda flinched at the words coming out of her mouth. She was getting way too handy with the fluid explanations, an art formerly practiced only by Charley. "Parker said you were close. He just didn't specify exactly what your relationship was."

"That's right," Teresa agreed. "He, uh, said you were very close."

Lila reached for another cigarette. "Yeah, we were. Do you have a problem with that?"

Ross looked at Teresa and arched his eyebrows in a questioning expression. She shrugged. Parker wasn't being as informative as they had hoped.

"Let me handle this," Charley said. "Parker, my man, were you and this lady..." He paused then cleared his throat. "Were you and this lady, uh, you know, sleeping together?"

Amanda could only imagine what crude expression he'd almost used. Actually, she probably could imagine it but didn't want to.

"Hey," Charley continued, "it's okay if you were. I mean, we're all adults here, right?" He paused and looked puzzled. "You weren't sleeping with her, and she wasn't blackmailing you. So you were paying her every month just because you're a nice guy? That doesn't make sense."

Naturally Charley found it hard to believe that anyone would have purely altruistic motives. Though, to be honest, Amanda didn't quite buy into that either. Something strange was going on, and both Parker and Lila seemed reluctant to discuss it.

Parker had been anxious to get his accounts transferred into Ross' name. That would make sense if she'd been blackmailing him. If she had been, of course Lila wouldn't want to admit it, but why wouldn't Parker speak up, exact revenge from the grave as Charley had done?

"So Parker was your friend and he helped you." Ross knelt next to Lila's chair and took the hand that wasn't holding the cigarette. "Can you help him now? Do you know anybody who'd want to hurt him?"

Lila took another puff of her second cigarette and smashed it in the ashtray with a vengeance. She wiped her eyes with the heel of her hand, smearing her mascara. "I thought you wanted to talk about Parker, not question me like you're a cop and I'm a suspect or something."

"She is a suspect," Charley muttered. "I bet she's still using. That's why she's wearing long sleeves in this weather, to cover the tracks on her arms."

"I'm asking as his brother," Ross said hastily, "not as a police officer. Just as somebody who loved him and misses him terribly, the same way you do. Someone who wants to see his murderer punished."

Lila rubbed her arms. "I don't know anybody who'd want to hurt him. Can we talk about something else?"

"Of course. The last time Parker came up for the weekend we went out and had a couple of beers, and he told me all about his classes. Did he tell you about the English class that was a required subject and how much he hated it?"

Lila relaxed visibly. "Yeah, he said he didn't understand why a geology major needed to read Shakespeare."

"I'm glad he got to see both of us one last time. You must have been the friend he said he was going to visit when he left my place Sunday two weeks ago."

She nodded. "Yeah, he came by for a little while on his way back to school."

"Was that the last time you saw him?"

Lila's eyes narrowed. "Yes."

"She's lying," Charley said.

"Yes," Amanda said softly. "I recognize the signs. Thank you for the training."

She spoke in a whisper, but Lila looked over at her, tears dry, dark eyes squinting. "Who are you talking to?"

"Myself. Nobody." She cleared her throat. "Bad habit. You smoke cigarettes, I talk to myself."

"Parker was doing really well in school." Ross skillfully drew Lila's attention back to the subject at hand. "Was it hard on your friendship, not seeing him often? Did he call you from school?"

She nodded.

"When was the last time he called you?"

"I don't remember." She focused on picking a bit of ash off the sleeve of her blouse.

"Lying again," Charley said. "This is getting really monotonous. I'm going to look through the rest of the house and see what I can find while that woman tells lies and you all pussy foot around."

Amanda shot to her feet. "You can't..."

He vanished through the wall before she could finish her admonition against snooping.

All eyes turned to her.

She coughed and sank back to the sofa. "Talking to myself again. Don't mind me. Just go on as if I wasn't here."

Lila's expression said she thought both these strange women were...strange.

"He gave you money every month," Teresa said, "so you wouldn't have to worry about working, so you could recover because you were on drugs." The last part of the sentence sounded like a question and Amanda suspected she was fishing, that Parker hadn't said that. Teresa was relying on Ross' information about Lila's drug arrests and Charley's belief that she was using again or still.

Lila glared at Teresa. "He had plenty of money and he wanted to share. He was a nice man." She didn't deny the accusation of drugs.

"Did he ever bring Steven Anderson to meet you?" Ross asked.

Lila's gaze shifted to one side. A slight flush spread over her cheeks.

Amanda vaguely recalled watching some crime show where the detective said looking to the left meant the person was getting ready to lie, right meant they were going to tell the truth. Or was it vice versa?

"No," Lila said.

"But you know who he is," Ross continued.

"Of course I do. The senator's son. He's dead."

"Did Parker try to help him get off drugs too?"

Lila blinked twice and reached for her cigarettes again.

"It helps to have somebody else in your same situation," Ross said casually. "Talk about what you're going through, help each other with the bad times. Steven had a few of those. His dad had to bail him out of jail more than once. But maybe he couldn't stay clean the way you did. Maybe Parker had to give up and walk away from him. Did he ever talk about Steven?"

She lit her third cigarette, her complete attention on the action, took a puff and shook her head. "No."

Teresa tilted her head toward the television as if listening then turned her attention back to Ross. "She's telling the truth."

"Of course I'm telling the truth!" Lila smashed her cigarette so hard, ashes from the first two flew upward.

Ross looked dubious.

Amanda felt dubious.

Charley darted back into the room. "Holy crap! You need to see all the papers in this chick's night stand. They weren't sleeping together! She's his sister!"

Chapter Eleven

Teresa spun and faced the television again. "She's your sister? Why didn't you tell me that?"

Lila shot to her feet. "One of you talks to the television and the other one talks to herself! There's something wrong with both of you!"

"You're our *sister*?" Ross deep voice rose several octaves on the last word.

"Says so right on her birth certificate," Charley affirmed. "Father, Nicholas Minatelli."

Lila looked at Ross for a long moment. Different emotions played across her face—fear, happiness, anger. Defeat won the struggle. She sighed and shook her head. "No." She fell back into the chair. "I'm Parker's sister, not yours."

Ross sank onto the edge of the coffee table. If it hadn't been there, he would likely have fallen straight to the beige carpet.

Teresa moved to sit beside him. "Her birth certificate lists Nicholas Minatelli as her father."

Ross peered at her closely, silently, digesting the meaning of her words. "Dad? My father—my stepfather is her father?" He spoke slowly, carefully. He'd totally lost his cop façade. "I don't understand."

"How do you know about my birth certificate? Did Parker tell you that too?" Lila gazed at Teresa as if she was an alien...or a ghost.

"Yes," Teresa said softly. "He told me."

"Actually," Charley said, "I told you. Give credit where credit's due. Parker just didn't deny it." He looked at the television screen. "Come on, man, give us more information. So your dad fooled around a little on your mom. It happens. It's not like you have to wear a hair shirt for what your old man did. You sure didn't have to pay out all that money."

Amanda would not have expressed it in exactly those terms, but Charley had a point. Protecting his deceased father's memory was one thing, but if Lila was twenty-six and Parker was twenty-one, the deed had been done before Parker was even born. In fact...

She looked at Teresa and tried to remember the exact details of the marriage of Ross' mother and stepfather. Had she said two years before Parker was born?

"Who are you? Why would he tell you?" Lila demanded.

Charley got directly between them. "He didn't tell her. I found the papers in your bedroom." He pointed to his chest. "Me!" He threw up his hands and sat on the coffee table next to Teresa. "It sucks when people ignore you."

Teresa laid a conciliatory hand in the general vicinity of his leg before turning her attention back to Lila. "I'm a friend he could talk to when he couldn't talk to anybody else."

That was, Amanda thought, a tactful way of saying she was conversing with Parker's spirit because no other living person could.

Lila frowned. "If you knew that all along, why would you ask me if we were sleeping together? That's sick! You're sick! I don't want to talk to you people anymore."

Ross leaned toward her, eyes narrowed, elbows on his knees, hands fisted. Back to cop mode? No, the air of desperation gave sincerity to his actions. He was genuinely distraught. "Please," he said. "I need to understand. My father never mentioned you. Who was your mother? Did Dad know about you? Did he take care of you? How did Parker find you?"

Lila's gaze narrowed. "If Parker told you everything, why are you asking me questions?"

"He didn't tell us everything." Teresa leaned forward, mirroring Ross' actions though she appeared more composed. "All we know is that you're Parker's sister. His half-sister. Now he's dead and won't...can't tell us the rest of the story."

"That's all Parker said, that I'm his sister?"

Teresa looked at the television and sighed. "Yes."

Lila lifted her tea, peered at it as if she wished it was something stronger, and took a drink. She set it half on and half off the coaster, her mind no longer on the preservation of her new furniture. Her hands shook as she lifted the package of cigarettes, took out another one and lit it then drew on it so hard the end sizzled.

Charley floated over to join Amanda on the sofa. "Parker just asked Teresa not to do this to Lila."

"How touching," Amanda murmured. As determined as Parker was to protect his sister, she probably hadn't killed him but she might know who did.

"So your mother had a relationship with Parker's father?" Teresa prompted, ignoring Parker's request.

"Mama worked at his pizza place. When I was little, she'd take me with her because she couldn't afford a babysitter. I'd sit in the back room and play." A ghost of a smile flickered across her lips. "Watch TV, color. Sometimes he...Mr. Minatelli...would come back and talk to me. He bought me toys and ice cream." She took another long drag on her cigarette and stared into the distance as if she too might be seeing ghosts. "I didn't know he was my daddy. I just thought he was a nice man."

"He was," Ross said softly. "He was a very nice man. He raised me as if I was his own son."

Any hint of a smile disappeared into a black hole. "Well, how nice for you. He didn't do the same for his own daughter." She focused her accusing gaze on Ross. "When he married your mother, she fired my mama because she didn't want the competition." She spat out the words.

Ross studied her intently as if he would see inside to her very soul and ferret out the truth. Finally he drew in a deep breath and shook his head. "I vaguely remember when my mom and dad got married that he had a woman working for him who had a little girl, but she had brown hair like her mother."

Lila nodded. "Dark like my mother and my father." She tossed her hair and raised a hand to smooth it. "I like being blond. When I look in the mirror, I just see me. I don't see my mama or that man."

"When did you learn that Nick Minatelli was your father?" Teresa asked.

"A year ago Mama died from lung cancer. She never would tell me who my daddy was. She said he was somebody rich and one day he'd come for us. He never did, of course. After she died, I was going through her things and found my birth certificate." Her lips thinned to a straight line. "And then it all made sense."

Her mother died from lung cancer? Lila bleached her hair so she wouldn't look like her mother, but the way she was smoking, she seemed to be trying to get lung cancer like her mother.

As if she could read Amanda's thoughts, Lila took another long drag on her cigarette and blew out the smoke defiantly. "We were dirt poor. I didn't have nice clothes and my mother struggled to pay the bills. We didn't always have enough to eat or a warm place to stay in the winter. All she knew was waiting tables, and that doesn't pay very much. I got pregnant in high school but I knew we couldn't afford to keep the baby. I gave it away." She glared at Ross as if the entire situation was his fault. "A little girl."

"Parker has a niece?" Ross spoke so softly Amanda could barely hear him.

"Yeah, that's right. Because my daddy threw away his daughter, he's got a granddaughter out there somewhere that none of us will ever know. While Mama and me were living on food stamps and I was buying my clothes from Good Will, my daddy was rich. He could have spent just a little of that money on us. He'd never have missed it, but it would have made a big difference for us."

"Did my brother find you or did you find him?" Ross asked.

"I tracked him down."

A muffled ringing sound came from the vicinity of Lila's butt. She pulled a cell phone from her back pocket and checked the screen. Her face went pale. She glanced at Ross then answered the phone. "I'll call you back. I'm busy now." Even from across the room Amanda could hear someone shouting on the other end. Lila swallowed hard. "I know. I got company right now. Parker's brother is here...I will...I will!" She returned the phone to her back pocket. Her fingers shook when she lifted her cigarette to her lips again.

Amanda and Teresa exchanged glances. Amanda would really like to know who had just called, who caused Lila to look so flustered and guilty.

"You found your brother, Parker," Ross reminded her.

"Oh, yeah, Parker. He was easy to find. We poor people don't make the news. We live on the outside. We're invisible. Nobody knows about us." She stabbed her cigarette toward Ross. "But you rich people, everybody knows about you."

"Amanda, I don't want you to get the wrong idea," Charley said, "but I think I need to find out who called Lila." He darted to the general vicinity of Lila's cell phone—her back pocket.

Amanda flinched and tried to look away but the spectacle held her attention like a bad automobile accident.

Lila frowned and wriggled uncomfortably as Charley slid around and through her derriere.

"You found him and extorted money from him?" Ross asked.

Lila expelled another massive stream of smoke and lifted her chin. "He gave me money to ease his guilty conscience. I'm entitled to that money just as much as he is."

A smiling Charley finally emerged from his visit to Lila's cell phone.

Amanda raised her eyebrows in a questioning manner. "Who?" she mouthed silently.

He shrugged. "I don't know. Her butt's in the way. I can't see anything."

He'd certainly taken long enough to reach that conclusion.

Teresa giggled.

"You think that's funny?" Lila asked.

"No." Teresa cleared her throat and waved a hand in a negative gesture. "No, of course not. I wasn't laughing at you."

Lila and Ross watched her expectantly.

"It's the same affliction that makes her talk to televisions," Amanda said. Another fluent lie. "She laughs when nothing's funny."

116

"I do," Teresa agreed. "Sorry."

Lila took out another cigarette though one still burned in the ashtray. Back to her faithful friend, Mr. Nicotine. "I don't mind talking to you," she said to Ross, "but your friends make me nervous."

He nodded. "I understand. Maybe I could come back another time without them."

"Yeah, I guess so, but I don't have anything else to say."

Ross stood and placed a hand on her shoulder. "What about our brother's estate? Don't you think you should be entitled to your share? When he died, his accounts all transferred into mine. The automatic payments to you have stopped. That's something we need to talk about. I can't change all the years you lived in poverty, but I can help to make your life easier now."

Time stopped. Amanda held her breath. Even Charley stood motionless, his feet a couple of inches off the floor.

Was Ross being sincere? When had he changed from accusing her of extorting money from Parker to offering her a share of Parker's estate?

"That's real nice of you," Lila said.

"We'll just do a simple DNA test and I'll see that you get half of Parker's estate."

Lila lips compressed and she shook her head firmly. "Parker already helped me. I won't be greedy."

"Ha!" Charley snorted. "She has *greed* written all over her face. I know greed when I see it."

Of course he did. He'd seen it plenty of times in the mirror.

Lila rose, shaking off Ross' hand. "Y'all need to leave now."

"I'll let you know about funeral arrangements," Ross promised.

"Thank you."

The three of them—four, if you counted Charley—filed out the door to the front porch.

After stilted good-byes, Amanda, Teresa and Ross walked across the yard toward the car.

Charley looked around. "Parker's not here. I'll go get him." He disappeared into the house.

The three non-spiritual entities drove away from the squatty brown house with its new furnishings and peculiar occupant.

Charley darted back into the car. "He won't come. He says he's going to stay with her for a while. Says they have unresolved issues."

Parker must have said it. Charley wouldn't use words that long.

Ross turned from the gravel drive onto the road. "I didn't expect that."

For a moment Amanda thought he meant he hadn't expected Charley to use those words either. Of course he was referring to Lila's blood relationship with Parker.

"Neither did I," Teresa said.

"He didn't tell you?" Ross asked. "He didn't give you any clue before we got there that Lila was his sister?"

"None."

"He didn't give you any clue *after* we got there." Charley intruded between Ross and Teresa in the front seat. "If I hadn't been there, you'd never have found out."

"I was a little surprised when you offered to share Parker's estate with her," Teresa said.

Ross shook his head. "I wanted to see how she'd react when I suggested the DNA test. I'm not sure I trust her. If Parker's been giving her money because he wants to make things right, why was he so determined for me to cut off that money, to get everything in my name? And why wouldn't she want it to continue if she has a valid claim? She doesn't have a job. He's been supporting her. Is she going to go back to being a waitress? A hooker? All she had to do was agree to take a DNA test and she'd be set for life."

"You don't believe she's really Parker's sister?" Amanda asked.

"I saw her birth certificate," Charley protested.

"Parker believed it," Teresa said. "Otherwise he wouldn't have given her money."

"Parker was very trusting," Ross said. "I'm not. If she was Dad's daughter, he'd have taken care of her. I'm going to find out what's going on, how she scammed him."

"Unofficially, of course," Teresa said.

Ross shrugged. A hint of his old smile reappeared. "Of course."

The visit hadn't been a total waste of time. Ross seemed to believe Teresa really was talking to his brother. Whatever happened with the weird Lila Stone, Teresa's relationship with Ross had benefited.

☙❧

The sun was below the tree tops when they got back to Teresa's apartment. Shadows softened the evening. It had been a long day. Amanda almost looked forward to collapsing on her uncomfortable sofa. Even better, maybe Jenny and Davey had reconciled. Maybe she'd have her bedroom back.

She climbed out of the car and stretched.

Ross wrapped an arm around Teresa's waist. "Thank you both," he said. "I've learned a lot today." He held Teresa tighter and smiled down at her.

"You're welcome."

Amanda reached inside the car and retrieved her helmet. The sun was low and would be directly in her eyes at some point during the ride to her apartment, but other than that, it was a perfect evening.

"Don't leave yet, Amanda," Ross said. "Let me take you all to get some burgers or a pizza or something."

Teresa cocked her head to the side and regarded him with raised eyebrows. "Now that we know how much money you have, you could take us out for steaks, not burgers."

Ross laughed. "We can do that. Where would you like to go?"

"Thank you," Amanda said, "but I really need to get home and see how my sister's doing."

"You mean you need to get home and see if she's still there or if we finally have the place to ourselves again," Charley said.

120

Have the place to ourselves. When *ourselves* included Charley, Amanda would never have thought she'd be happy to hear that phrase, but at the moment, it didn't sound so bad. Better than sharing the apartment with both Charley and her sister.

"I'll take a rain check too." Teresa was refusing to go to dinner with Ross? "Talking to spirits is a very draining experience." She lifted a hand to her forehead. "I just want to have a glass of wine and crash."

For a moment Ross' face darkened. Was he going to say something about Teresa's casual reference to talking to spirits? He shook his head and gave a mock grimace. "Did I just strike out with two women in one night?"

"Check with me tomorrow. I promise to repair your ego."

"Good night." Amanda slid on her helmet and moved toward her motorcycle.

"Wait!" Teresa called. "I have your earrings that you forgot the other day."

She probably wasn't talking to Ross.

Amanda turned back. "No, you don't."

"Yes, I do. Come in and get them." Teresa stood on tiptoe and gave Ross a quick kiss. "Tomorrow."

He got in his car and started the engine.

Teresa took Amanda's arm. "I know you didn't leave any earrings at my place," she whispered. "But I need you to stay." She waved and smiled at Ross as he drove away.

This best friend stuff could definitely take a toll. "Why do you need me to stay?"

"We need to find out who called Lila while we were there."

Amanda withdrew her arm. "No, we don't."

"Yes, we do," Charley agreed. "She totally freaked out when she got that call. The guy on the other end yelled at her, and she let him get away with it. Something's going on with that."

"Ross wants to know more about her," Teresa said. "He's starting to accept my abilities. This is my chance to prove it. I don't have to say which spirit told me about the phone call."

"Charley looked around her cell phone quite thoroughly, and he couldn't see anything except her butt. Parker's not going to tell us. Why don't you just let Ross subpoena her phone records?"

"He can't. He's on leave, remember? He can't be connected with his brother's case, and all those other people that Senator Anderson's going to bring down will find it first if we don't hurry. We need to go out there and let Charley have a look around. Besides, Parker may still be there and maybe Charley can get more information out of him."

"Great idea," Charley said. "I want to check out her bedroom some more."

Amanda looked at him.

"For more documents!"

Teresa clasped her hands. "Please? You and I don't even have to get close to the house, just close enough Charley can go in."

Amanda had not forgotten the time she did that very thing at Mayor Kimball's house. That had not turned out well.

"We'll be in and out in ten minutes. I'll drive really fast to get us there, and the whole thing won't take more than an hour. Then you can go home and see your sister."

Hang out in the weeds at Lila's house while Charley explored or head home immediately and listen to her sister. Neither choice held a lot of appeal.

Amanda sighed. "All right. I'll do it." This best friend thing could definitely be stressful.

Chapter Twelve

They crossed the parking lot to Teresa's convertible sitting in the shelter of covered parking.

"Can I drive?" Charley asked then laughed. "Just kidding." The wistful expression on his face said he hadn't been kidding. Charley had been a fan of fast cars, fast motorcycles and fast women. Now he was without all three.

Amanda waved a hand at the car. "We can't take this. Parked along that farm road, it'll stand out like a race horse in a herd of mules. We'll have to take my bike. It's black and small enough we can hide it off the road."

Teresa's eyes widened. "Your bike? You want me to ride on the back of a motorcycle?"

"When we first met, you said you'd always wanted to learn to ride one."

"Well, yes, but I didn't mean I wanted to ride on the back of one."

Amanda gave a slight shrug. "I've ridden in your car. Riding on my bike can't be scarier than that."

"I like riding with her," Charley said.

Teresa arched an eyebrow at him. "You've only ridden as a passenger on her bike since you've been dead. If you were still alive, you'd fear for your life."

Amanda lifted her hands, palms outward. "That's my offer. Take it or leave it. I'm not really excited about this trip anyway."

"I don't have a helmet."

Helmets weren't required by law in Texas, but it would be foolish for Teresa to ride without one. "You got a bicycle helmet?"

"An old one from high school."

"Go get it. Change those slacks for jeans and those sandals for something sturdier, something more weed-worthy."

Ten minutes later Teresa returned wearing tight jeans and cowboy boots with inlaid patterns. Her hair was tucked up under a bicycle helmet that looked as if it would be better than nothing...but not a lot.

Amanda climbed on her bike and Teresa got on behind her.

Charley settled between the two. "This is going to be fun, just like the time you took me to Kimball's house so I could look around for evidence. We had a good time, didn't we?"

"Yeah, if you think having handcuffs slapped on your wrists and being threatened by a psycho is a good time, I had a great time." She pulled down the faceplate of her helmet and started the bike.

Only half the sun blazed above the horizon as they headed south for the second time that day. It would be almost dark by the time they got to Lila's house. A good thing. The area didn't have a lot of trees to hide behind.

125

Amanda got as close to Lila's house as she could, then stopped and lifted her faceplate. A few gnarled mesquite trees and clumps of weeds dotted the barren landscape, but it was twilight and getting darker. They should be able to do this. The moon was barely a quarter, and they would be out of there in ten minutes.

Amanda pulled the bike next to a tree where it almost blended in.

Charley darted happily toward the house.

Amanda started through the brush.

Teresa hung back. "This is close enough, isn't it?"

"Come on!" Charley called. "I'm almost inside! You need to move a few feet closer."

"Does that answer your question?" Amanda asked.

Teresa shivered. "Okay, all right. I guess if she decides to shoot us, Charley will warn us." She looked at Amanda. "Won't he?"

"Oh, yeah, Charley's a great security system."

"Are you being sarcastic? I never know when you're being sarcastic."

"Come on!" Charley motioned them forward.

Amanda turned and began crunching through the underbrush.

"You're not leaving me alone!" Teresa followed close behind.

When they reached the edge of Lila's yard, Amanda stopped behind one of the larger mesquite trees. With its gnarled limbs and scant but still-intact foliage, it provided decent cover.

Charley gave them a thumbs-up and disappeared inside.

Teresa wrapped her arms around herself though the evening was warm. "So you've done this before?" she asked softly.

"Yeah, Charley and I went to this guy's house one night so Charley could search it. It was the man who murdered Charley."

"What happened?"

"The man had security gates and cameras and the whole paranoid setup. He knew the minute we broke into his gates. He called the cops and let us wander around until they got there. I don't think Lila's likely to have any of that stuff."

Nevertheless, she scanned the branches above for a hidden camera.

"She's got the windows open and the lights on," Teresa said. "We can see right inside her house. We should have brought binoculars."

"That's what Charley's for. He explores and reports back to us. You don't want to tell Ross what you find out from peeping in Lila's windows. You want to tell him what the spirits find out for you, right?"

"I guess so. I feel strange, just standing here in the dark." Teresa shifted. "Ow!"

"Sh-h-h-h! With the night this still and her windows open, she could hear us."

"Damned tree stabbed me."

"There's a reason they're called devil trees. Keep your voice down. Remember, she might have killed Parker. She may have a gun."

"You're right. We don't want to get too close to the house. Look, she's getting undressed." Teresa pointed at a window toward the back of the house.

Lila was definitely pulling off clothes. "I bet Charley's enjoying that."

"What is she doing? It's too early to go to bed."

"I don't know. Maybe she has company, and they're planning to do things that require them to be undressed."

Teresa shook her head. "There's only room for one car in her carport. If she had company, there'd be another vehicle in the yard."

"She's probably going to take a shower." Amanda shifted her gaze to another window, away from Lila's progressively more nude body.

"She really is skinny," Teresa said. "I can see her ribs from here."

"That's not an image I want to take home with me."

"She's doing some kind of a dance, spinning in front of the mirror and laughing."

Against her better judgment, Amanda looked at Lila. She was indeed writhing in front of the mirror in a provocative manner. Charley would definitely be enjoying that. "You don't think she's getting ready to have sex with Charley or Parker, do you? I mean, is that even possible?"

"No!" In the gathering darkness Amanda couldn't see Teresa's face, but she could hear the eye-rolling in her tone. "Well, I don't think so. Oh, she's getting dressed again. Something red."

"Short, red, and tight. I'm pretty sure that's not a night gown. She must be expecting company."

"Or going out."

Amanda squinted, trying to see more of Lila's bedroom. "You're right. We should have brought binoculars."

"I'll remind you to do that next time we're spying on somebody." Teresa shrieked, ducked and waved her hand in front of her face.

Amanda cringed. Teresa's scream had split the quiet of the night.

"Something attacked me!"

Lila looked briefly in their direction then went back to dressing, adding a sparkly necklace to her evening ensemble.

"Be quiet," Amanda cautioned. "It was only a bat. He wasn't attacking you. He was just getting that mosquito on your nose."

"You're making that up, aren't you?"

"The mosquito part, yes. Where'd she go? I don't see her."

Maybe she was coming outside to investigate the noise. Maybe they should leave.

Lila reappeared, rising as if from a sitting position on the floor. She looked down for a long moment. Finally she sighed and walked out of range of the window.

"That was weird," Teresa said.

"This whole thing is weird. Look, Charley's coming through the side of the house."

"And Parker's right behind him."

"We gotta get to the bike!" Charley shouted as he darted up to them, his form glowing faintly in the gathering darkness. "She just picked up her car keys. She's leaving!"

The light went out in the bedroom.

"Why don't we just stand here in the shadows and wait till she's gone?" Amanda asked.

Charley shook his head. "We have to go with her."

Amanda gave him a scathing look. "No, we don't."

"Yes, we do," Teresa said. "Parker says we need to find out what she's up to."

"We only need to know who that call was from. Charley, did you find out?"

"Yeah, it was Stanley Wagner."

Amanda frowned. "The same Stanley Wagner, brother of Clyde, the guy out target shooting by the well where we found Parker's body?"

"I don't know." Charley pointed to the house. "She's leaving."

Lila walked across the front porch and headed for her carport.

"The woman's obviously got a hot date," Amanda said. "So what?"

Charley held out his hands in a supplicating manner. "Parker says we have to go with her. He's worried about her. He said she did some meth just before we got here."

Amanda sucked in a sharp breath and looked at Teresa. "Did Parker really say that?"

"Did you?" Teresa tilted her head and looked at the air. "Yeah, her source of income is gone, and she's back on drugs. He's worried she might also be going back to her old trade."

"Her old trade? I assume he's not talking about being a waitress. I don't think the waitresses in the Waffle House wear outfits like that."

"Prostitution," Teresa affirmed. "He wants us to find out and if she is, stop her from doing it."

Amanda rubbed her forehead. "And just how do we go about this? Have a stern talk with her? Threaten to put her in time out?"

Lila's white sedan pulled out of the carport and headed down the road.

"She's getting away!" Teresa charged into the brush, heading toward the bike. "Come on! The way you ride, you can catch her if we leave now. Let's go!"

Charley looked toward the empty space between Teresa and him. "Okay, okay!" He sighed. "Parker says *please*. Just follow her and see what she's going to do. Be sure she's all right."

"I think she passed the *all right* stage when she did meth." Amanda threw her hands up in resignation. "Fine, we'll follow her, but I want it on record that I do not think this is a good idea."

Amanda reached her bike first and pulled it onto the road. "Helmets on and let's roll."

Soon the three of them—make that four since Charley and Teresa vouched for Parker's presence—caught up to Lila's car on the highway, heading toward Dallas. At least they'd be closer to home when this crazy run was over.

Lila took Woodall Rogers Freeway and turned into the downtown area.

Amanda had expected her to head for a different area, but amidst the downtown night life such as homeless people and drunks, there were some luxury hotels probably crawling with luxury prostitutes. Maybe one of them was her destination.

Lila turned down a dark alley. No luxury hotel in sight.

Amanda rode past then parked on the street. Surely no cops would be coming by at this hour to give out parking tickets. And if they did, oh well, a parking ticket was no big deal. Didn't raise her insurance rates like speeding tickets.

She killed the engine. The world became suddenly and eerily quiet.

"This is a scary part of town," Teresa whispered.

Amanda pulled off her helmet. "You wanted to follow her."

"Don't worry. I'll take care of you ladies," Charley said.

"That's very reassuring." He could send a cold chill through an attacker or make their cell phone go wonky. Not exactly traits treasured in a bodyguard. Amanda hung her helmet on the handlebars. "You want to help? Go see what she's doing in that alley."

Charley curled his lip. "I don't know if I want to see."

"I do." Teresa slid off the bike.

Amanda grabbed her arm. "One minute you're scared and the next you want to rush headlong into a dark alley?"

Teresa shook off her hand. "I didn't say I was scared. I just said this is a scary part of town."

"Whatever. I don't think we want to get caught spying on this woman when she's doing whatever it is she's doing. Let Charley and Parker go. She can't shoot them."

"Come on, buddy," Charley said, encouraging the air to follow him.

He—they—disappeared around the corner, into the alley.

A man across the street waved. "Hey, ladies, looking for a little action?" He smiled, revealing a few gaps in his teeth, then staggered slightly as if tripping on the jeans that hung loosely on his thin hips.

Amanda shook her head vehemently and motioned for him to go away.

He dangled a small plastic baggie.

"Is that meth?" Teresa whispered.

"I have no idea, and I don't want to find out."

Charley darted back around the corner. "She's sharing her drugs with some scuzzy guy. He doesn't look like he can pay very much for her services."

"She probably doesn't charge much." Teresa flinched. "I'm sorry, Parker. I shouldn't have said that. I know you care about her. I know she's your sister." She turned to Amanda. "He's pretty upset to see that she's apparently...well, you know."

Amanda straddled her bike. "I know more than I want to know. Let's get out of here. Now."

"Good idea." Teresa got on behind her.

Amanda lifted her helmet above her head...and Lila came around the corner with a man in tow.

Lila's eyes widened in recognition.

Busted!

Amanda slammed on her helmet, started the bike and roared away.

Damn all the one way streets! She rarely went downtown and made several wrong turns before she finally got back on the freeway.

Okay, so Lila had seen her. What was she going to do? Amanda had no intention of turning her in to the cops for using drugs or for solicitation. She wasn't a threat to Lila.

Nevertheless, she was perspiring by the time they pulled into Teresa's parking lot.

"She saw Amanda," Charley said.

"Lila?" Teresa asked.

"She was probably so wasted, she won't remember." Amanda hoped she was so wasted she wouldn't remember.

Teresa looked at the empty space beside her. "I'm sorry, Parker, but I don't know what we can do." She listened for a minute then pulled off the bicycle helmet, shook out her hair and turned to Amanda. "He wants us to try to help her. He says she's suffered enough and underneath it all, she's a good person, someone who can be redeemed."

Amanda wasn't feeling a lot of sympathy for Lila. "Short of kidnapping her and hiding her in a cave in the middle of Big Bend National Park, I don't know how we're going to stop her from doing whatever she wants to do."

Teresa nodded. "Go home. I'll talk to Parker."

Home. What a beautiful word after their crazy day.

"You ought to call your sister," Charley said. "She'll be worried. She's probably already called the cops, the FBI, the CIA and your mother to report you missing."

The beautiful image of home evaporated.

Even so, it was better than spying on a meth head prostitute in an alley in downtown Dallas.

Amanda checked her watch. A little after eleven. "Jenny'll be in bed by now. I don't want to wake her."

"Chicken," Charley accused.

"If I call her now, we'll be on the phone for an extra hour. Get on the back. We're leaving." She groaned. "What am I saying? You can't get on the back. You're just a..."

Charley settled on the passenger seat. "There's no need for name calling."

"Good night, Teresa." Amanda flipped down her faceplate.

The ride home was familiar and only a few miles. She usually enjoyed riding at night, but now the inky darkness hid unknown terrors, transformed benign trees, street signs, and toys left on lawns into strange creatures. She couldn't decide if this onset of panicked delusions was caused by their visit to the underbelly of society or by the thought of dealing with her sister for another night.

When she turned into her parking lot a few minutes later, her sister's Mercedes was still there.

"Guess she hasn't gone home to Davey," Charley said. "If she waits much longer, that baby's going to come and you can learn how to change diapers."

Amanda pulled her bike into the shop, yanked the key from the ignition and slid off. "Shut up." She closed the shop door behind her and tromped upstairs.

"Amanda's going to be an auntie!" Charley sing-songed. "A hands-on auntie! Ah, the sound of little feet pitter-pattering across the floor and the smell of spit-up."

Amanda jerked open the door of her apartment.

Jenny struggled upright from the sofa and yawned. "Hi, Amanda. I must have fallen asleep waiting. I'm so glad you're home." She waddled toward Amanda, arms extended for a hug. "I was getting worried about you. You keep really strange hours. Well, I guess you always had that tendency. I remember when Mother caught you trying to break into the house at two o'clock in the morning."

Amanda returned the hug in spite of a vivid memory of that occasion. Jenny had deliberately locked the window she'd gone out of and expected to return through.

"Did you see Davey?" Amanda asked. "He's very worried about you."

Jenny's hand moved to the diamond necklace that sparkled at her throat and a smile started on her lips, but she pursed them and looked stern. "Yes, he came by and we talked."

"I see he speaks her language," Charley said.

"And?" Amanda encouraged. "Did you work things out?"

Jenny turned away and crossed the living room. "We're going to meet for lunch tomorrow and discuss things."

Charley groaned. "*Discuss things*? What does that mean? More jewelry?"

"Lunch tomorrow." That meant another night on the sofa, but maybe only one more. Her tone when she talked about him didn't sound quite as hostile as before.

"Did he tell you Steven Anderson's body was found?" Surely the thought of being involved in the pomp and ceremony of a funeral would send her flying homeward.

Jenny assumed her sad expression. "He did. That's so awful. Davey said he'd take care of sending flowers and our expressions of sympathy. He doesn't want me to get involved in all that since I'm pregnant." She sighed. "Just one more thing I can't do because I'm pregnant."

"Maybe he doesn't want her to come home," Charley said. "You'd think he'd know her well enough to use the funeral as bait."

Though Amanda had been thinking sort of the same thing…in a nicer way, of course…she frowned at Charley.

"I have something to show you." Jenny's expression changed to a smile and she waved a hand toward the bedroom door. "I wanted to do something to thank you for taking me in and being there when I needed you, so I redecorated your bedroom."

Charley darted into the bedroom then out again, his expression horror-stricken. "Don't go in there, Amanda."

Chapter Thirteen

Gone was the faded patchwork quilt that had rested quietly and unobtrusively on her bed for the last three years. Also gone were the two happily mismatched garage sale lamps on her mismatched night stands. A purple patterned comforter lay across the bed. Silk scarves covered the nightstands and blended with purple shades on small matching lamps. The purple theme continued in various hues throughout the room...on the dresser, the chest of drawers, throw rugs and new drapes that covered the antique blinds.

"I know how much you like purple." Jenny stood beside her in the doorway. "What do you think?"

Charley burst into gales of laughter. "I wish you could see the look on your face! If you puke right now, it'll be purple."

Amanda turned to look at her sister and made a concerted effort to twist the corners of her mouth upward. "It's...uh...thank you for...uh...doing all this work. You shouldn't have." *You really shouldn't have.* Amanda tried to think of something gracious to say about the room. *It's lovely. This is so nice.* She couldn't bring herself to tell such outrageous lies. "How did you do all this when you can barely walk?"

"Why, I paid the decorators at the store to do it, of course. But I picked out everything myself."

It's the thought that counts. "That must have been a lot of work. Uh, where did you put my quilt?"

"Oh, it's in the closet. It seemed clean enough and I thought you might need the extra cover this winter. I don't think you have very good insulation in these walls."

It's the thought that counts. It's the thought that counts. "What about my lamps? They generate heat. Be good this winter in this drafty old place." Amanda could hear the sarcasm dripping from her voice. Thoughts counted, but so did actions.

Jenny giggled. "You're so funny, Amanda. I had to throw those awful lamps away. The wiring looked dangerous. I'm surprised you haven't burned the place down already."

"I found them at garage sale and rewired them myself."

"Garage sale? Well, no wonder. These lamps are new and the wiring is UL approved. You can sleep soundly tonight and won't have to worry about a fire." Jenny pulled back the spread and revealed lavender sheets. "Thousand thread count. Your old ones were very scratchy. Tonight you can snuggle in, relax, and get a good night's sleep." She smiled and spread both hands toward the bed.

Amanda took a step backward. "I can't sleep in that bed. I mean, you can't sleep on the sofa in your condition. No, you have to sleep here tonight. I'll sleep on the sofa again." Jenny hadn't invaded the living room.

Yet.

She waved a hand dismissively. "I bought an air mattress that the salesman guarantees is as comfortable as any regular mattress. All I have to do is lay it out on the floor, plug it in, and it fills itself. It's the same height as a regular bed. I may have to get you to bend over to plug it in and put on the sheets." She looked down at her protruding abdomen. "I'm so clumsy now. Do you remember how I used to dance?" She lifted her arms as if planning to do a pirouette, then sighed and dropped them back to her sides. "I can't dance anymore. I can barely walk. Now I understand why the grocery stores have special parking spots for pregnant women. We should have handicapped stickers for our cars. Of course, Davey usually takes me places and lets me out in front of the door."

Amanda's spirits rose in spite of the damage to her bedroom. Jenny sounded a little wistful when she talked about Davey. They were meeting for lunch tomorrow. One more night. If she could get through one more night.

A rapid knocking on the front door interrupted her fantasy. "Maybe that's Davey." *Please be Davey, come to take Jenny home!*

She started toward the door, but Jenny laid a restraining hand on her arm. "Of course it's not Davey. It's after ten. Davey would never knock on somebody's door at this hour. I don't believe I know anybody who'd come to call so late."

"I have an idea," Amanda said. "Let's open the door and see who it is."

Jenny's hold on her arm tightened. "It's dark out there and you live in such a bad part of town. I don't think you should open that door."

The knocking sounded again, this time in a faster rhythm as if the caller was growing impatient.

"I'll go see," Charley said. He darted through the door then back. "It's Lila."

"Lila?" Amanda repeated, her heart rate accelerating. "What's she doing here?"

"Lila?" Jenny echoed.

"Uh, yeah, Lila."

"How can you tell before you open the door?"

"I recognize her knock," Amanda improvised. "We don't want to talk to her. Don't answer."

"I should say not. How rude to arrive at this hour."

"You better open this door!" Lila called. "I know you're in there. Why were you following me?"

Jenny's eyes widened. "You were following her? Who is this woman?"

Amanda shrugged as if the incident were of no importance. "Just...a friend of the brother of a friend. She's delusional." All true.

"I think we need to call 911." Jenny released Amanda's arm and moved toward the coffee table, toward her purse.

Amanda stepped between her and her goal. "No, let's don't do that." She was pretty sure she hadn't broken any laws by following Lila but she didn't want to explain the situation to the cops, especially not to Jake and Ross.

"Go away!" Charley shouted.

Amanda wanted to shout the same thing. Instead she crossed the room and stood next to the door. "What do you want?"

"I saw you!"

"Yeah, well, I saw you too. So what?"

"You don't know what you're getting into." Lila was no longer shouting. Her words were soft and her voice trembled.

"Amanda, what's she talking about?" Jenny stood next to the coffee table, one hand clutching the side of her face and the other rubbing her stomach. "What's happening?"

Amanda's eyes widened. Was Jenny going into labor? "What do you mean, what's happening? Why are you rubbing your stomach?"

"She's having the baby! Lila's scared her into labor!" Charley cowered against the door next to Amanda.

She gaped at him in horror. What did he expect her to do?

"Amanda," Jenny said, "I think—"

"No!" Amanda held out a hand, stopping the words as if she could stop the action. She whirled around and opened the door far enough to confront Lila. If Jenny was having the baby, they didn't need a crazy woman blocking their way to the hospital. "Go away!"

Lila weaved slightly on her red stiletto heels. Her eyes were bloodshot, her pupils dilated. Drugs. She clutched a red bag in one hand and pointed a long red fingernail at Amanda with the other. She leaned so close Amanda could smell her stale cigarette breath and something else, something acrid and chemical. "Stay out of this. Stay away from me and keep your mouth shut about whatever you think you saw tonight."

In spite of the woman's bad breath, Amanda leaned toward her, adopting an aggressive posture she didn't feel. "I don't care how much meth you take or how many men you sell your body to. My sister's having a baby. Get off my property now!"

"I'm calling the police!" Jenny shouted from inside the room.

"No!" Lila opened the red bag, fumbled inside, and withdrew a small revolver.

Amanda froze.

"Gun!" Charley shouted and dove for cover somewhere behind Amanda.

"You don't call the police and you don't come around me again." Lila fumbled with the gun and managed to get one finger inside the trigger guard. Her hand shook so badly, even if she fired, she might miss her target...or she might not.

Amanda slammed the door in Lila's face. "Get down!" She lunged across the room and grabbed Jenny who shrieked as Amanda tugged her out of the line of fire and onto the sofa.

"What's going on?" Jenny demanded, struggling to sit upright. "Why did you grab me like that? Who is that woman? I knew you shouldn't have moved to this neighborhood. Mother says you weren't safe. Daddy owns some rental properties in a nice area up in Richardson. You could move into one of those."

Jenny rambled on as Amanda watched the door. No bullets ripped through the flimsy wood. Lila was no longer shouting threats. Jenny was babbling but said nothing about a gun. Thank goodness she hadn't seen that part.

"I'll get rid of her." Charley darted through the door.

Jenny tried to rise but Amanda held her back. "Just a minute. Let's wait for..." She couldn't say, *Let's wait for Charley to report back*. "For just a minute. To be sure she's gone."

Charley returned. "She's leaving. She brought that man in her car, the one from the alley. He's totally wasted. He was staggering around your parking lot when she went down, but she shoved him into the car and drove away."

Amanda released Jenny's shoulder and stood. Great. Lila had not only brought her gun, she'd brought her john along for the late night visit.

Jenny pushed to her feet and tugged on Amanda's arm. "Are you listening to me?"

"Yes...no...Jenny, are you in labor? Is the baby coming now?"

Jenny shook her head. "No. Why would you ask that? Of course, having that crazy woman at the door was enough to cause a miscarriage. I was so scared! We need to call the police. She might come back. Do you have people like that coming to your door often? Have you talked to that detective who came home with you the other night? I'm sure he's not happy about the kind of neighborhood you live in."

"Jenny, can you be quiet for just a minute?"

145

Jenny dropped Amanda's arm and crossed hers over her protruding abdomen. "I guess I can. Excuse me for worrying about my big sister. It's not like you make good decisions. You married that awful man and now you live in this awful place."

"You married an awful man? Were you married to somebody before me?" Charley asked.

Amanda pressed her hands to the sides of her head. "I need everybody to stop talking and let me think!"

Jenny backed away. "Everybody? Amanda, there's nobody here but me. Are you saying I'm talking enough for two people? I was just trying to help. I didn't mean to get you all upset. But, really, all I've been saying is for your own good."

Amanda sucked in a deep breath and lifted her hands in a placating gesture. "I'm sorry. It's been a long day. I'm really tired. I think we should go to bed now."

Jenny's eyes rounded in astonishment. "You want to go to bed after what just happened? How can you possibly sleep after that?" She lifted a hand to her chest. "My heart is pounding. Does this sort of thing happen so often you get used to it?"

Getting Jenny to go to sleep was the only way she could think of to shut her up. Putting a gag in her mouth wasn't really an option. Maybe, if she wasn't pregnant...

But she was.

"Yes," Amanda said firmly. "I'm exhausted. I would like nothing better than to go to bed." She collapsed onto the sofa and turned her face to the back.

"But...what about your new bedroom? Don't you want to sleep in there tonight? I can blow up the air mattress and sleep in here. You'll be more comfortable in your own bed, though your mattress doesn't have a lot of support. You really..."

Amanda emitted a loud, phony snore.

"Oh my. I guess she really was tired. I don't think I'll sleep a wink after everything that's happened. But of course she can sleep. She's not pregnant." A long sigh trailed away as Jenny's footsteps left the room. "It feels like I've been pregnant all my life. I don't even remember what it's like not to be pregnant."

The bedroom door closed.

Thank goodness for small favors.

"She's talking to the sheets," Charley reported. "Telling them how smooth they are."

Amanda ceased the faux snoring, rolled over and sat up. She couldn't put Charley to sleep.

"What do you think was going on with Lila?" he asked. "I wonder how she found you. I mean, sure, Ross introduced you this morning and she saw you tonight on your motorcycle, but she doesn't seem smart enough to track you down."

"Well, she did," Amanda whispered. "I own a business. I'm not hard to find. The real question is why?"

Charley shrugged. "You came to her house with a cop, and you saw her tonight committing a crime. You freaked her out."

"Then we're even. She freaked me out. But when she said I didn't know what I'm getting into, she sounded more scared than threatening."

"Sure she's scared, scared of going back to jail. It's not a fun place to be. That gun she had sure looked threatening."

Amanda shook her head. "She didn't know what to do with it."

"She managed to get her finger on the trigger. From there, it's pretty easy to do something with it."

"I guess." She sat for a moment staring into the darkness. "It doesn't make sense."

"Of course it doesn't. She's a nutso junkie."

"I agree with that part. But she's lost her supply of money. She's forced to go back to work, whatever form that may take. So why did she share her drugs with that man in the alley? He didn't look like he could afford her services, however cheap those services may be. And then she loaded him into her car and brought him along with her when she dropped by to threaten me in the middle of the night. I don't get it."

"I told you, she's a junkie. They do strange things."

"What about Parker? He's not a junkie. He's obsessed with taking care of her, but he was also obsessed with cutting off her supply of the family money. If she's his sister and he doesn't want her to go back to drugs and prostitution, why not just keep quiet and let the automatic payments continue? If he hadn't led us to his body, who knows how long it would have been before anybody realized he was dead, especially with somebody sending text messages from his cell phone?"

"Yeah, that was weird, getting messages from his phone when he was in the room with us."

"Had to be his killer." She looked at the bedroom door, assuring herself it was still closed and Jenny wouldn't hear her talking to herself about murders. "I don't suppose you saw an extra cell phone lying around when you were going through Lila's house?"

He shook his head. "Just hers. The only calls she had recently were to and from Stanley Wagner. She got some meth from somebody. Could be from him."

"We saw her get down on the floor. Was she so high she fell?"

"I don't know. She just suddenly dropped to her knees and ran her hands over the rug. It's a really ugly rug. You know how everything else in that house is new? Well, she's got an old rug in the bedroom that has faded flowers on it. Maybe it was her mother's and it has sentimental value."

"Maybe, but she doesn't seem like the sentimental type to me."

The bedroom door moved, opening.

Amanda fell back onto the sofa and closed her eyes.

"It's your sister," Charley said.

What a surprise. Who else would be coming out of her purple bedroom?

"Omigawd! She's going to smother you with your own quilt!" he said.

Jenny draped something over Amanda, tucked her in with gentle hands, and left the room.

Just when Amanda was ready to strangle her and feel no guilt for the act.

Why did people have to be so complicated?

Jenny made her crazy. Threw away her lamps. Criticized her home. Changed her home. Then tucked her in.

It was hard to have pure feelings of anger at her sister or even at crazy Lila. Lila's life had not been easy, and now, after a brief period of financial freedom, she was going back to taking drugs and selling her body. What was she doing with the drugged guy from the alley? Taking him home with her? That made no sense.

Amanda had gone through a lot of jobs before settling on motorcycle repair, and most of that time she'd been short of funds. But she'd always had the safety net of moving in with her parents. She'd never once considered that option, but she would have done it rather than sell her body—assuming she could find any buyers.

Jenny had proclaimed melodramatically that she and her baby would have to live in a hovel, but that would never happen. She had Davey to take care of her. Worst case scenario, she had her parents.

Lila had no safety net.

Amanda lay on the sofa, warm and cozy under the quilt for a long time before sleep finally came.

Amanda tried to sneak out of the apartment before Jenny woke the next morning, but when she stepped out of the shower, her sister was sitting on the bed in her voluminous nightgown. "I bought some bagels and cream cheese yesterday. We can toast them and have a nice breakfast. You can drink your Coke, but hot tea would be better. I bought some onion bagels and some cinnamon, so you'll have some variety."

"Thank you. That sounds wonderful, but I don't have time. I'm late for work." Amanda threw on her clothes, grabbed a Coke and ran down the stairs with Charley close behind.

"That's not a healthy breakfast," Jenny called from the doorway.

"I don't think I've ever seen you eat a bagel for breakfast," Charley said. "Leftover pizza, tacos, toaster waffles, but not bagels."

"They're okay if you pile on enough flavored cream cheese." Amanda opened the door to her shop and went in.

Dawson looked up from the motorcycle he was working on and pushed his glasses higher on his nose. "Amanda, have you talked to Jake? Is he all right?"

Amanda stopped. A cold chill darted down her spine even though Charley hadn't touched her. "Jake? No. Why wouldn't he be all right?"

Dawson rose slowly. "You haven't seen the news?"

She shook her head. That cold chill spread through her chest. "No. I don't watch the news. It's too depressing."

Dawson rubbed the back of his head and compressed his lips. "Guess I'll have to be the one to depress you. Yesterday evening the sheriff's department down south in Kraken County went to question some elderly man out on a farm with regard to the bodies found on his property. He opened the door and started blasting with a shotgun. The sheriff took him prisoner but the guy who went with him was shot. They haven't given out a lot of details, but they said Dallas County Detective Jake Daggett was taken to the Kraken County General Hospital. That's your Jake, right?"

Amanda licked her dry lips. "Yes," she whispered. "That's my Jake."

Chapter Fourteen

"*Your* Jake?" Charley's eyes widened, and his expression turned grim.

"Did they say how badly he was hurt?" She held her breath.

Dawson shook his head. "All they said was that he was taken to the hospital. Want me to find out?"

"No. I need to see for myself."

"See for yourself? What does that mean?" Charley planted himself directly in front of her, hands on his hips. "You want to see him injured and bleeding? I don't think that's a good idea."

Amanda pushed through him, her insides already so icy she didn't feel the usual chill, and strode toward her motorcycle on the far side of the work area. "I'll be back in a couple of hours," she called over her shoulder.

"No problem," Dawson replied. "It's a slow day. I hope Jake's okay."

Charley followed close behind. "Where are you going? So he got shot. That happens to cops. Goes with the territory. Part of the job description."

Amanda grabbed a leather jacket from a hook and a helmet from a shelf.

"Think about what you're doing," Charley ordered. "You're not going to go down there to see him, are you? If he wanted to see you, he would have called."

Amanda hesitated, helmet half on. It was true. He hadn't called her. He'd been shot yesterday, taken to the hospital, and he hadn't called her to let her know.

But what if he couldn't talk? What if he was in a coma? What if...?

Pushing the bone-chilling thoughts aside, she shoved her helmet into place and fastened the chin strap. She could see Charley's lips moving but his words were muffled by the helmet. It provided safety in more than one way.

Within minutes she was speeding down the highway, heading toward Kraken County Hospital...toward Jake.

Maybe Charley was right. Maybe he'd have called her if he wanted to see her.

It wasn't like they had a real relationship. They'd only gone out a few times. Only kissed a few times.

But they were significant kisses, meaningful kisses.

She cursed the traffic. Perhaps the other drivers weren't in a hurry to get somewhere but she was. What if she got there too late? What if he...

No, she wouldn't think about that.

She hit the gas and darted around two sedans, going between the lanes of traffic, a very unsafe practice. Her handlebars cleared the vehicles by inches. Charley appeared in her peripheral vision, shouting something she couldn't hear.

After what seemed like a journey half way around the world, she turned into the hospital parking lot, pulled off her helmet and fastened it to the sissy bar.

"Are you crazy?" Charley demanded. "You know better than to ride between cars like that! You could have been killed. What were you thinking?"

She strode across the concrete to the hospital entrance.

Charley stood in front of the door, hands outstretched. "I can't let you do this, Amanda."

She pushed through him for the second time that day.

He followed her. "That was really rude. Do you have any idea what it feels like to have somebody walk right through you? I hope you never find out, Amanda. It's not a good feeling."

A receptionist sat behind a large desk.

"What room is Jake Daggett in?" she asked.

"Two fifteen. Second floor, halfway down on the right."

The woman had given her a room number. That meant he was still alive. Amanda crossed the area to the elevator and pushed the *up* button.

"You shouldn't be wandering around a hospital," Charley said. "There's all kinds of germs here. You could catch something and end up dead, and it's not as much fun as you might think."

The elevator doors opened.

Charley stepped in front of her, his brows lowered in a fierce scowl. "This is not a good idea."

Amanda halted with one foot inside. The elevator was electric. Charley had abilities with electrical equipment. "Is that a threat?"

"What?"

"Are you planning to strand me halfway between floors?" Amanda spun on her heel and headed for the stairs.

"Of course...I...I...how can you say that?" Charley's sputtering attempt to deny the accusation, to lie, told her she'd hit on the truth. "If he wanted to see you, he'd have called you. Don't set yourself up for a fall."

If Charley really thought Jake didn't want to see her, would reject her, he'd be encouraging her to hurry.

One flight of stairs, down the hall on the right.

Room two fifteen.

At the door she hesitated. Swallowed. Sucked in a deep breath. Knocked on the wooden frame of the open door. "Jake?"

"Amanda?" His deep voice was slow and groggy.

She stepped into the room. The crooked smile on his face dispelled all fears. He was alive. He was glad to see her. She felt her own lips move upward in response. "Hi."

Lying on the hospital bed with tubes connecting him to various machines and a huge white bandage on his left shoulder, he still looked strong and vital.

He licked his lips and cleared his throat. "I got shot."

"I heard."

"Come in." He motioned with his right hand to a plastic chair on the other side of the bed. His IV trailed along with the gesture. "Have a seat."

"Don't sit there!" Charley warned. "You don't know who's been sitting there. That chair could be covered with a million kinds of germs. You sit there and they'll be crawling all over you."

"Thank you." She crossed the room and sank into the chair. If she could deal with Charley, she could certainly handle a few million germs.

"Good to see you." Jake's voice croaked and he cleared his throat again. "They put tubes down my throat when they knocked me out last night to get the slugs. Throat hurts worse than the bullets."

"Yeah, about those bullets... What happened?"

"Oh, good grief!" Charley flipped a hand through Jake's injured shoulder.

Jake flinched and shivered, made a rough attempt at laughter then coughed. "Okay, maybe the throat doesn't hurt worse than the shoulder."

"I've had all I can take of this." Charley left the room. He was sulking again. She'd have a few minutes of privacy.

She leaned closer to Jake. His right hand lay on his chest. She wanted to take it in hers, feel his warmth, reassure herself he was still alive and breathing. She folded her hands in her lap to restrain any such impulsive impulse. "What happened?"

"All hell is about to break loose. Senator Anderson is pulling every string he can to find out what happened to his son. They're working on warrants for everything you can imagine. In a day or two the property around that well will be swarming with law enforcement. The man who owns that property is Lloyd Carstairs, a man Laskey's known most of his life. His dad was best man at Carstairs' wedding. Now the guy's eighty-five and getting a little senile so Laskey wanted to talk to him first. Since he was doing it kind of under the table, he let me go with him instead of one of his deputies."

Amanda waited.

Jake blinked slowly. Was he going to sleep? He was wounded, in the hospital. He probably needed his sleep. She should go and let him rest.

But if he dozed off then woke and found her gone, that might be stressful for him. That justification meant she should stay.

She cleared her throat.

His gaze focused on her and he smiled. "Hi, Amanda."

"Hi, Jake. Carstairs," she repeated. "You went out to question Carstairs. Isn't that the guy those deer hunters thought called the cops on them for trespassing?" Stanley Wagner was one of those deer hunters. Was this another link to him?

"Yeah, Carstairs calls the sheriff a lot. His wife and daughter were killed by an intruder about thirty years ago, and he went a little nuts after that. Claims to see intruders on his property and in his house. Sometimes it's those Wagner boys, sometimes it's

President Truman, and sometimes it's strangers. Laskey has to check out all the calls, but they never find anybody."

Another reference to those Wagner boys. Should she mention Lila's phone call with Stanley Wagner? If she did, she'd have to explain how she knew. That wouldn't be easy without admitting Charley got the information for her. Besides, Jake was recovering from a bullet wound. She shouldn't bother him with details that might be meaningless. It might not even be the same Stanley Wagner. "So a senile octogenarian put you in the hospital?"

Jake laughed then coughed again. "Yeah, but let me tell you, his bullets hurt just as much as bullets from somebody younger. Laskey said he was a good man, a little crazy but harmless. He greeted us at the door with a twelve-gauge shotgun. I took a couple of pellets of double-ought buckshot in my shoulder. I don't think he's such a good man and certainly not harmless."

Amanda shivered at the image Jake's words conjured in her mind—the powerful projectiles thrusting into his body, sending jolts of pain through him, releasing the red blood of life from his veins. "You were lucky you only got hit by two of them."

"From that close range, if he'd been a better shot, I'd be..." He paused, looked at Amanda, then looked away. "I'd be a lot worse off."

He'd be dead. That's what he'd started to say. Amanda swallowed. And if he died, he probably wouldn't come back like Charley did. Not that she wanted Jake to be in that state. She wanted him alive and warm and on the same physical plane she was. "Did Sheriff Laskey get hit?"

"No, the rest of the load went into the tree behind us. He took down Carstairs, handcuffed him and arrested him."

"I'm glad you're not...you know...hurt worse. Though I guess having two slugs in your shoulder and having those slugs dug out is pretty painful."

"With all the drugs they've given me, not so much."

Jake was on drugs, heavy-duty drugs. That explained why he was so relaxed, why he was telling her so much and not just spouting that line about not being able to talk about an on-going investigation. Maybe she should leave. Not take advantage of his drugged state. Yes, that's what she should do. She'd verified that he was alive, that he was glad to see her. Now she should leave.

He smiled at her. "Hi, Amanda. I'm glad you came."

He was confused, thought she'd just arrived. It would be rude to leave now when he thought she'd just come. She should stay and visit a while. And if he wanted to tell her details of the crime, it would only be polite to listen.

"So Carstairs murdered Parker and all those other men in the well?"

Jake made a movement she interpreted as nodding. "Allegedly." It took a couple of attempts before he got the multi-syllable word right. "Man's got an arsenal, every kind of gun from twenty-two revolvers to deer rifles, and he shot an officer."

"That he did," Amanda agreed. "He shot you."

"Looks like most of the bodies were killed with a rifle, but they matched the bullet that killed Parker to a Glock found in a kitchen drawer in Carstairs' house."

"That's pretty damning. I'm glad they caught Parker's killer. Any idea why he did it?"

"He claims he's innocent. They all say that. But he admitted he had those guns to protect himself from the people trespassing on his property and breaking into his house. We can only speculate that Parker was on his property, Carstairs saw him, thought he was an intruder, and shot him."

"Maybe all those calls he made about trespassers were real people, but he killed them and dumped them in the well before the sheriff's department got there to answer his calls."

"Maybe. Or maybe he killed them and called the sheriff when their ghosts came back to haunt him." He chuckled at his own joke.

Ghosts. Sensitive subject. Her conversation with Jake was going so well on so many levels, she wasn't sure she wanted to get into the ghost thing. However, he was on drugs. How much of this conversation would he even remember?

"You mean a ghost like Ross' brother?"

His face settled into rigid lines for a moment, then he relaxed and looked confused. Good drugs. "I don't know what to think of that story. Do you?"

She shrugged noncommittally, unwilling to admit that she could vouch for the truth of it because she had her own personal ghost. "Teresa has a gift."

"She did take us to Parker's body," Jake conceded. "But if she really could talk to him, why didn't he tell us who killed him?"

"I don't know. There's a lot I don't understand about ghosts."

"I guess it doesn't matter since finding the body led us to Carstairs, so in a way he told us. If she really talked to him." He lifted a hand to his forehead. "Thinking about that makes me dizzy."

It was probably the drugs that made him dizzy, but she wasn't going to argue. "Does Ross know?"

"Yeah. He called. He's the one who told me about the match on the bullets. He was really happy about finding his brother's killer. His brother's alleged killer. He took Parker's death pretty hard."

"I know he did. Any idea why Parker would have been lurking around Carstairs' place?" Had he ventured onto Carstairs' property while following Lila in an effort to stop her from doing something he didn't approve of? Did that something involve Stanley Wagner?

"Don't know," Jake said. "We don't even know where he was killed. The well was a secondary crime scene. Parker's body was moved."

"Oh, yes, Parker said something about his journey out there when he didn't realize he was dead."

"Parker said?" Jake's eyes narrowed and his gaze sharpened.

Uh oh. If she knew which gadget had the pain meds, she could give it a little bump to be sure he stayed dopey. But she didn't. The best she could do was change the subject. "The other bodies, were they killed somewhere else too?"

Jake's eyelids drooped.

Amanda cleared her throat again. "The other bodies? Any idea who they are?"

Jake's eyes opened and focused. "The decomp is so bad except for Parker and Steven Anderson, it's going to be tough to figure it out. Anderson was involved in drugs and the other bodies have bad teeth. That happens a lot with meth users. This could all be about drugs."

"Drugs? It's hard to picture an eighty-five year old man snorting a line of coke or trying to find a vein to shoot up."

Jake gave a lopsided grin. "That's not exactly what we were thinking. Could be somebody's cooking meth on his property. Middle of nowhere, elderly man who rarely gets out. It would be a perfect place. That might explain the people he sees."

Lila used meth. Stanley Wagner could be her dealer, and the possibility this was the same Stanley Wagner they'd met was increasing. He could even be the one cooking meth on Carstairs' property.

That did it. She had to tell Jake what they'd discovered about Lila's phone call. She cleared her throat and tried to come up with the best way to phrase it. "I have reason to believe that Lila Stone may know Stanley Wagner." That sounded way better than, *My ex-husband's ghost found calls between Lila and Stanley when he swept through her phone after she got upset over a call that came in while I was at her place with Ross and Teresa.*

Jake blinked a couple of times. "Lila Stone? Who's Lila Stone?"

Apparently the cops hadn't found that connection yet. "Parker's...umm....it's a long story. We'll talk about it later." She'd tried to tell him. She'd done her duty. She rose. "I guess I better leave and let you rest."

He smiled and reached for her with his good hand.

She took his hand in hers.

"I'm going to have a couple of weeks off when I get out of here before they'll let me go back to work. Maybe we could go somewhere together. It'll still be warm on Padre Island."

Amanda's heart soared.

"Just the two of us," he said, "get away from all the crazy stuff around here."

Her heart sank. *Just the two of us* would be great but not possible. She'd have to take along her ghostly chaperone. Nevertheless, she smiled. "I'd love that."

He tugged her closer.

She leaned toward him. Her lips touched his. Even on drugs, he was a great kisser.

"Carstairs didn't do it!" Charley shouted. "Hey, what's going on? What are you doing?"

Chapter Fifteen

Amanda jerked upright, thrust in one instant from the delicious warmth of Jake's lips to the sharp cold of Charley's presence.

"I leave you alone for one minute and come back to find you cheating on me." Charley glowered, his face a study in rage.

Jake blinked in confusion. She could only hope he was so drugged he wouldn't remember this aborted kiss.

"I'm glad you caught Parker's murderer," she said. "Hope you get to go home soon."

"Can you get a move on?" Charley stood just inside the doorway, motioning her out. "Parker's all in a tizzy about an innocent man being arrested."

Amanda squeezed Jake's hand. "See you later."

His smile put the warmth back in her heart. "I'm glad you came by."

She brushed past Charley into the corridor. "Not so innocent," she whispered. "He shot a police officer."

"Yeah, well, defending a man's freedom and property from a cop who's not even in uniform is a far cry from being blamed for killing six people."

There was no point in trying to correct Charley's deliberate perversion of the facts about the shooting. "They have evidence that incriminates the man."

A nurse coming down the hall gave Amanda a quizzical look.

If living with Charley didn't get her sent to the psych ward, talking to him in public was going to. Just one more thing to add to her list of complaints against him.

Charley lifted his chin and looked down his nose. "Parker says he didn't do it, and Parker should know who killed him."

Amanda rolled her eyes and went through the door to the stairs with Charley close behind. "So Parker says it, and that settles things? Why doesn't Parker just come to Carstairs' trial and testify that he's innocent? That should clear up everything."

Charley's forehead furrowed. "He can't do that. Nobody can see him except Teresa and me."

"Still haven't got a handle on sarcasm, have you?" Amanda went down the stairs then pushed through the revolving door and outside into the fresh autumn air, a major improvement over the stale hospital air.

A slender woman with dark hair rushed toward her, a slender woman she knew well.

Amanda stopped and blinked. "Teresa?"

"Thanks for coming out. I hated to interrupt you and Jake, but Parker insisted. He's very upset."

Amanda looked at Charley then back to Teresa. "What's going on?"

"Didn't Charley tell you?" Teresa blew out a long sigh. "Parker says Carstairs didn't kill him."

"Yes, he told me that part. He didn't tell me you were here. How did you know where to find me?"

"Charley and Parker. They've joined forces, heaven help us all. Ross and I were having a really good time what with the mystery of his brother's death solved and no reason to talk about ghosts." She slid an annoyed gaze toward her right. Amanda assumed Parker was there. "But then Parker came in and started nagging at me to tell Ross that Carstairs is innocent. Have you ever tried to be romantic with a ghost nagging at you? Well, yes, I guess you have. When I ignored him, he ran off to find his new best friend." She scowled at Charley. "He returned knowing how to turn the lights and TV on and off and make the volume loud enough for the neighbors in the next county to hear. Thank you, Charley, for teaching him all those wonderful things."

Charley smiled.

"He's not good with sarcasm," Amanda said.

"That was sarcasm?" Charley looked offended.

Teresa looked frustrated. "Anyway, it was either get into an argument with a ghost in front of Ross or send him home. Ross, I mean. I wish I could send the ghost home."

Amanda spread her hands in confusion. "Okay, you sent Ross home without telling him about Carstairs. That didn't make Parker happy. But why are you here?" She had a feeling she knew why, but in case she was wrong, she wasn't going to give Parker any ideas.

"You're next on the list. He wants you to tell your police friend—his words—that Carstairs didn't kill him in spite of the evidence because the victim's ghost, speaking through me, says so. He wants to start this whole thing all over. Ruin my relationship with Ross again."

Amanda shook her head. "Not happening. Even if my police friend wasn't lying in the hospital, wounded, on drugs...which he is...I wouldn't tell him that. They matched the bullet that killed Parker to one of Carstairs' guns."

"Yes, Ross told me all that. He's very relieved they found his brother's killer." She flinched and lifted her hands to the sides of her head. "Okay, okay, I understand he didn't kill you, Parker. Let me rephrase that. Ross is very relieved because he thinks they found his brother's killer. He's become his old self and our relationship is back on track." Again she looked to her right. "At least, it was."

A couple walked out of the hospital and glanced in their direction.

"Let's go sit in your car to discuss this," Amanda suggested.

They walked across the lot to the blue convertible parked beside Amanda's motorcycle.

"I'm glad you finally put the top up," Amanda said. "I don't really want to have this discussion in the open air where people can hear us and think we're nuts."

Teresa laughed, but the sound lacked her usual spark. "I agree." She slid into the driver's seat. "It's a little claustrophobic, but it's getting chilly, and claustrophobia beats talking to ghosts in public."

Charley floated down between them. He usually perched on the back of Teresa's car behind the seats, but with the top up, that spot wasn't available.

"A little crowded too," Amanda said. "I suppose Parker's here as well."

Teresa nodded. "He's behind me, half inside and half outside."

"Parker, even if the man didn't shoot you, he shot Jake and maybe those other men in that well. He's not an innocent man."

Teresa drew a hand through her hair and shook her head. "He's only concerned with the fact that Carstairs didn't kill him. I guess the other dead people are on their own."

"Parker, this is getting ridiculous," Amanda said. "If you want the cops to believe that Carstairs didn't kill you, you're going to have to tell us who did. Give them somebody else to investigate."

Silence.

Teresa shook her head again. "He refuses to say who his killer is, just that it's not Carstairs."

"Then we're done," Amanda said. "We're going to have to let the cops figure this out and come to whatever conclusion they come to."

"I'm afraid she's right, old buddy," Charley said. "The cops aren't going to pay any attention to your story. They're total dunderheads. Let them do their thing with Carstairs while we go grab a beer."

"You can't grab a beer," Amanda reminded him, "and the cops aren't dunderheads. When Carstairs—

or whoever—killed the senator's son and dumped him in that well with the others, they made a huge mistake. Jake said by tomorrow that place will be swarming with law enforcement officers from everywhere. They're working on the warrants right now. They'll gather evidence, take Carstairs to trial and let a judge and jury determine his guilt or innocence. That's the best we can do." She turned to Teresa. "We found Parker's body and Ross took care of his bank account. Isn't there a white light or something he needs to go to?"

Teresa gave a very long sigh. "That's the ultimate goal, but he says he can't leave if his death is blamed on an innocent man. We need to go with him to talk to Carstairs."

Amanda gazed toward the empty space behind Teresa. "Parker, Carstairs is in jail. I'm not sure he's accepting social calls."

"He says if we talk to him and Parker is convinced he's guilty of other crimes—"

"You mean like shooting a police officer?"

"That's a start, but he's thinking more like he might be guilty of shooting those other guys in the well. If he's convinced Carstairs is a murderer even though he isn't responsible for his murder, he says he'll try to move on."

"He'll *try*?" Amanda repeated. "That's not exactly a signed and notarized affidavit."

"It's better than nothing. Look, help me get Parker on his way so I can have a relationship with Ross, and I'll owe you a dozen evenings of babysitting Charley so you can be with Jake."

"Babysit me?" Charley folded his arms across his chest. "I won't go with you."

He had no choice, but Amanda wasn't going to argue with him. "If it works, fifteen evenings, one week continuous. If we do it but Parker doesn't leave, I still get ten evenings, five of them together."

Teresa frowned. "Five evenings in a row?"

"So Jake and I can take a trip together."

Charley flung his arms wide. "Nobody asked me if I agree to this! I don't!"

"Deal," Teresa said.

Amanda drew in a deep breath and slowly released it. "I used to lead a normal life until I married Charley. Now I'm sitting in a car, making deals that involve ghosts."

"At least you had a few good years. I've talked to them most of my life."

"If only I could find a way back in time. Instead of saying *I do*, I'd say, *No freaking way*."

"Hey!" Charley protested. "We had some good times."

"Well, you can't go back," Teresa said, "so I guess we're going to jail."

Chapter Sixteen

Amanda parked her bike beside Teresa's car in the small lot next to the Kraken County Jail in the middle of beautiful downtown Grackle, the county seat of Kraken County. In spite of the harsh sounding names, the town square was charming. Many of the original buildings from the turn of the century were still there including a courthouse, a bank that had become a jewelry store and a grocery store converted to an ice cream parlor.

Teresa slid out of the front seat. "I've been thinking about this. I'll go in as Carstairs' lawyer. That way we can be sure we'll get to talk to him."

She could probably carry it off. She looked regal and elegant in dark slacks and a blue pullover that matched her car. Amanda hadn't changed clothes. She still wore jeans, leather jacket and motorcycle boots. She ran a hand over her hair that had been under a helmet most of the day. That did nothing to help the frizz. She couldn't even pass for Teresa's assistant.

"You do know it's illegal to impersonate an attorney," Amanda pointed out.

"Only if I offer him legal advice. I won't do that since I don't have any to offer." Teresa opened the tall wooden door to the building and glided inside like a model on a runway.

Amanda, Charley and, presumably, Parker followed.

The place had been updated to the extent that one side of the room was walled off except for a large window that exposed a cluttered metal desk. A short, stout woman with short, stout gray hair rose from behind the desk and strode over to the waist-high window. "Help you?" she said into the microphone. A name tag on her beige uniform identified her as Deputy Alexander.

Teresa smiled.

Deputy Alexander did not. If only she'd been a man, she'd have been smitten with Teresa's smile and they'd have been in with no problem.

Charley darted inside the cubicle. Being rude and nosy again.

"We're here to see Lloyd Carstairs," Teresa said. "I'm his attorney."

Deputy Alexander crossed her arms over her chest. "Can I see some identification?"

Charley came out to rejoin them. "She's got about a bazillion pictures of kids on her desk. Must be grandkids."

Amanda stepped up to the window and edged Teresa over. "We're his granddaughters. I'm Amanda Caulfield, and this is Teresa Landow."

Deputy Alexander's eyebrows sank low over her dark eyes. "Why'd you say you're his attorney?"

"She is an attorney," Charley advised, "but right now she's just his grieving granddaughter."

173

"My sister is an attorney," Amanda lied smoothly, "but mostly she's his granddaughter. We haven't seen Granddad in years." She sighed. "It's so sad to be reunited under these circumstances."

Deputy Alexander put a fist on her hip. "That old man doesn't have any grandkids. His daughter was only sixteen when she and her mama were murdered."

Curse small towns where everybody knew everything about everybody.

"Your father was his son from his first marriage," Charley said.

"Our father was his son from his first marriage," Amanda repeated. She hated to take Charley's advice, but when it came to deceit, he was an expert.

Deputy Alexander's eyes widened. "Lloyd was married before? Him and Helen dated in high school!"

"Well," Teresa said, moving closer to the window, "he didn't exactly marry our grandmother. They just shared one night of passion when he was out of town."

The deputy's eyes grew even wider. "Lloyd?" She blinked a couple of times then stepped to one side and pressed a buzzer. "Go into the first room on your left. I'll bring him in." She shook her head. "Guess we've all got our secrets. Lloyd? Who'd a thought?"

Within minutes they were seated at a scuffed wooden table in a small private room with Lloyd Carstairs. He was a tall man and had probably once been well muscled. Now his flesh hung on him like an ill-fitting garment. A few strands of white hair decorated his large pink scalp. His head merged with a thick neck and, as he swung his head to and fro from Teresa to her and back again, he resembled a slow-moving bison. A bald bison.

Amanda held her breath, hoping he wouldn't denounce them as fraudulent granddaughters.

Teresa smiled. "Hi! I'm Teresa. I'm an attorney. Your attorney."

Carstairs clasped his manacled hands on the table and leaned forward, his expression guarded. Jake had said Carstairs was senile, but he might not be senile enough to believe these strange women were his granddaughters.

"I'm Amanda. Remember me?"

"She's your—" Teresa started, but Amanda laid a restraining hand on hers.

"You look like somebody..." Carstairs shook his head. "I don't know. Everybody looks like somebody I used to know, but they're all dead. Helen, she had hair like you." He rubbed his forehead. "No, she had golden hair, hair the color of wheat when it's close to harvest time. Who did you say you are?"

"I'm Teresa. Your attorney. You've been accused of shooting a police officer."

Carstairs snorted. "He wasn't a police officer. He was a trespasser. He was on my property, on my porch. I'm tired of people coming around all hours of the day and night, hollering and carrying on, keeping me awake." His voice was surprisingly strong and certain.

175

"Can you tell me about the people who trespass on your property?" Amanda asked. "Do you know the names of any of them?"

"Course I do. You think I'm senile or something? Them Wagner boys, they never were worth the lead it would take to shoot them. Their mother, Pearl, she was a fine woman, but their daddy run her off. I always wondered if she really left or if he killed her. He was mean. Never took care of that farm like he should have. Pearl waited on him and them boys hand and foot. She was a fine woman. You remind me of her." He stopped and looked confused. "No, she had blond hair. Or was that Helen?"

This wasn't working out so great.

"So the Wagner boys trespassed on your property?" Amanda asked.

"Didn't I just say that? They come skulking around all the time, them and their friends. They're too lazy to farm that land. Nearly lost it a few years ago. Then they started leasing it out to people who pay to come down here and hunt deer. They hunt deer out of season. They hunt my deer. It's not right to set around and do nothing and then let people pay to kill my deer."

"Have you ever seen them cooking the deer?" Except for what she'd seen in *Breaking Bad*, Amanda wasn't sure of the process for cooking meth, but if Carstairs had seen somebody cooking something, surely that would be a clue.

"No," he said, "but they messed up my kitchen. My Helen used to keep that place spotless. Now

176

those people come in and break dishes and spill stuff all over the place."

"Not in your kitchen. Outside. Did you see them cooking deer outside? Having a barbecue? Smoke coming from a van?"

He shook his head. "No, no barbecues. They just run around yelling, showing up at my door in the middle of the night naked, trying to fool me into letting them come into my house."

"Naked?" Amanda repeated. "Naked people come to your house in the middle of the night?" Could they trust anything this man said? Would Parker be able to leave based on the word of a man out of touch with reality?

Carstairs frowned, looked at the floor and shook his head. When he lifted his gaze, his eyes seemed clear and lucid. "One naked man. He pulled out chunks of his hair and scratched himself till he was bleeding."

So much for lucid. "But you didn't let him inside your house."

"I don't let anybody come in. My wife and daughter were killed by a trespasser last year."

Last year?

"I know," Teresa said. "I'm sorry. So these people that come around, are they the ones who killed your wife and daughter?"

Carstairs sat back in his chair and regarded Teresa as if she were an idiot. "That man went to prison thirty years ago. He's still there. I check regular."

In and out of reality.

Amanda drew in a deep breath and prepared to ask the important question. "Have you ever shot any of these intruders before last night?"

He nodded. "Sure. I shot a lot of them."

Success! Hand in her lap, Teresa gave her a *thumbs-up*.

"Did you shoot one of them with your Glock?" Amanda asked. Maybe he had shot Parker after all. Maybe dead men didn't always have accurate memories of dying.

"Glock? I don't own a Glock. I don't hold with those silly plastic guns. Give me a nice Smith & Wesson .38 revolver. But a man don't hunt with a hand gun. I killed a lot of deer with my Winchester Model 70. That's what I shot them trespassers with." He paused and looked puzzled. "The deer always bled, but those men I shot didn't bleed until that one yesterday. He got blood all over my porch. Helen won't like that. She keeps the place spotless. One time I tracked mud on that porch, and she got upset with me. She doesn't usually get upset with me. She's a good woman."

Teresa looked at Amanda and rolled her eyes. "So you shot people, but they didn't bleed?"

Carstairs laid his hands on the table and stared down at them as if he could find his lost sanity there. "I thought that man would just run away like the others did after I shot them. But he didn't. He fell down on my porch and bled and then that other man grabbed me and brought me here." He shook his head slowly. "Helen's going to be mad at me if I'm late for dinner."

"We might as well get out of here," Charley said. "This guy's crazy."

Carstairs lifted his head. "I am not crazy. I get a little confused sometimes, that's all."

Amanda's jaw dropped. She looked at Teresa who was having the same reaction.

Amanda turned back to Carstairs. "Who you're crazy?"

Carstairs flipped a hand toward the corner where Charley stood. "That man over there, the guy with the blond hair. Who is he?"

"It's my ex-husband."

"Husband," Charley corrected.

Carstairs laughed. "Reckon there's some question about that divorce."

Holy cow. Carstairs could see and hear Charley.

"What about that other guy?" he asked. "The one who hasn't said anything. What's your name? You look kind of familiar."

Could he see Parker too?

"Course I didn't kill you," Carstairs said. "If I'd killed you, you'd be wandering around my property, hollering and carrying on like the rest of them. Wouldn't be coming to see me in jail."

"Do you know that man?" Amanda asked tentatively. "The one who said you didn't kill him?"

"Of course I don't know him. He came with you. Don't you know him?"

"He's with me," Teresa said. "But you said he looked familiar."

Carstairs shook his head. "Everybody looks like somebody I used to know. Most of them are dead now, but that doesn't stop them from coming back. I wish Helen and Grace would come back. Helen came back but she didn't stay long." He smiled wistfully. "I was so happy to see her in the kitchen, pulling out a cabinet drawer, getting ready to cook just like she used to do. But then she left. I hope she comes back. Maybe next time she'll bring Grace with her. Are we through talking? I'm tired."

"Yes," Amanda said. "I think we're through."

Maybe the man wasn't senile after all. Maybe people thought he was because he saw ghosts. Maybe the men he shot–other than Jake–didn't bleed because they were already dead.

Chapter Seventeen

Amanda leaned against her motorcycle and looked into the distance, past the picturesque buildings of the Grackle town square, toward the orange October sun perched at the edge of the horizon. Darkness came earlier every day this time of year, and it would soon overtake them. "Looks like Parker may be right. I don't believe Carstairs killed him."

"I told you so." Charley stood next to Teresa, folded his arms and leaned a few inches into the side of Teresa's car. Was he deliberately or unconsciously mimicking Amanda's pose? "A man knows who killed him and who didn't, especially men like Parker and me. We know things that you people stuck on the earthly plane don't."

Amanda let that one pass. They had more important things to do than discuss Charley's ego. "I believe him when he said he doesn't own a Glock, that he's a revolver man, that he hates polymer guns. That's not uncommon for older men, and in that same vein, I can't see him sending those text messages that came from Parker's cell phone after Parker was dead. I doubt if Carstairs has ever used a cell phone."

"You're probably right," Teresa said. "Jake didn't mention finding Parker's cell phone in Carstairs' house?"

"No, but it could be there and they just didn't find it on that first search. Or maybe the murderer planted the Glock but kept the cell phone for some reason. Parker, do you know where your cell phone is?"

She waited.

Teresa sighed. "Guess what? He says it's not important."

"Parker, that's getting a little old. I think I'd like it better if you'd just say *no comment* or *none of your business*." Amanda clenched her fists then relaxed them. "Okay, that tells us his killer has his phone. And we will assume that person is not Carstairs."

"Even if Carstairs didn't kill Parker, he could have killed those other men in his well," Teresa said. "He admitted he'd been shooting people."

"People who didn't bleed." Amanda considered what Carstairs had said. "I don't know. I just can't see him being organized or sane enough to drag bodies to the well and dump them in."

"I can't believe you're taking up for him after he shot Jake. I'd think you'd want to see him punished."

"I do, and he will be. He shot an officer, and the senator's son was in a well on his property. Based on those two things alone, he's pretty much screwed. But the reason he shot Jake, the reason Jake and Sheriff Laskey came to his front door in the first place, is because somebody killed Parker and dumped his body in Carstairs' well. That same somebody could have planted the murder weapon in his house. I feel kind of sorry for that senile old man who lost his wife and daughter and then lost his mind. The person I blame for Jake being in the hospital is the murderer who caused all this."

"And there's nothing we can do about it since the murder victim won't tell us who really did it." She glared at the ice cream parlor. Either she'd developed a sudden distaste for ice cream or Parker was standing between her and it.

Amanda had to make a decision. She could go home now and wait for events to take their course, for the justice system to work things out, hope that Carstairs was only punished for the crime he actually committed. Or she could take action. "Actually," she said, "there is something we can do. If Carstairs shot men who didn't bleed and he saw his dead wife in the kitchen, there is one among us who may be able to communicate with the spirits of those men in the well, maybe even the spirit of the senator's son. They may not be as reluctant as Parker is to tell us who killed them."

Teresa stopped glaring at the ice cream place and blinked a couple of times. "You mean me?"

"You're the only medium around."

"That's not a bad idea. If I can get information from the spirits of the victims, we can prove Carstairs is innocent, Parker can move on into the light, and Ross will have to admit I have a talent, not a psychosis."

"I think a quick trip to Carstairs' house is in order. It's practically on our way home anyway." Amanda lifted her helmet.

Her cell phone rang. She lowered the helmet and took the phone out of her pocket.

Jenny. Oh, dear. She'd forgotten about her sister.

"Where are you? When are you coming home?" Jenny asked.

Amanda cringed. She wasn't accustomed to having someone monitoring her activities, waiting for her, demanding she come home at a certain time.

"I ordered lasagna with garlic bread and Caesar salad," Jenny continued, "from that wonderful Italian place over by me. They're going to deliver it. I had to pay extra for them to come to this neighborhood, but it's worth it."

"It's going to be about an hour. I have an errand I have to run first."

"Well, hurry! I can't wait to see you. I have a big surprise for you."

Amanda disconnected the call before her sister could continue the monologue. She drew in a deep breath and put the phone back in her pocket. "My sister has another surprise for me."

"Maybe she's redone the living room to match the bedroom." Charley smiled. Actually, he smirked. "Or maybe she's going to choose a different style. Maybe you'll return home to deer heads on the wall with a coffee table of moose antlers sitting on a bear skin rug." He laughed uproariously at his own joke.

"I wonder if it's possible to have a ghost's head stuffed and mounted on the wall." Amanda jerked her

184

helmet on, covering her ears to block the sounds of Charley's laughter.

As she followed Teresa's car to the highway, she fancied she could feel the weight of a ghost on the bike behind her. It was a heavy weight.

The road leading to Carstairs' house had once been gravel, a treacherous surface for a motorcycle, but over the years dirt and mud had settled around the bits of stone. The ride was bumpy and uncomfortable but not dangerous.

Yellow crime scene tape glowed in the faint moonlight as they approached the place. Teresa parked with the hood of her car under the tape, and Amanda came to a stop beside her.

Like its owner, the house was big and old and not well cared for. The white paint was peeling and one of the shutters on the tall left window dangled precariously. The railing on the wide wooden porch that wrapped from the front around one side was missing a few rails and needed paint. Weeds shared the yard with grass that probably hadn't been mowed or watered all summer. A large magnolia tree on one side and a live oak on the other spread wide limbs all the way to the roof.

Charley leapt off the bike, darted directly through the tape and looked around. "I don't see anybody. How about you, Parker?"

Teresa stepped out of her car, lifted the tape and ducked under. "I don't see anybody, but I can feel another energy. Somebody's close. Let's walk into the woods in the direction of the well."

185

Night was settling around them, and the dark woods didn't exactly beckon invitingly. "Maybe if we wait a few minutes right here, one of them will come by," Amanda suggested.

"Scared there might be ghosts in those woods?" Charley laughed again.

"Shh!" Teresa waved a hand at him. "I think I see something. Somebody."

"Hi!" Charley bounced up and down, waving wildly. "I'm Charley! I can see you!"

"Are you one of the victims from the well?" Teresa asked.

"You already know him, Parker?" Charley sounded a little disappointed. "Oh, well, yeah, I guess spending time in a well together would make for a bonding experience."

"I'll see that your sister knows what happened to you," Teresa said. "Lacy Patterson in Waco, and you're Grant Patterson. Got it." She turned as if to face another spirit. "Mark Randolph. Okay."

"I know you!" Charley pointed into the darkness. "You're Senator Anderson's son. You were in the well."

Teresa nodded. "I'll tell your father how sorry you are that you caused him to worry and that you're okay now."

As Amanda listened to Charley talking to the spirits and Teresa repeating the names then making promises to contact loved ones, she felt like the new kid on the playground, left out of the *in* group. "Who killed them?" she finally asked.

Teresa listened then frowned. "A hunter? A deer hunter?" She tilted her head. "I don't understand. A hunter shot you? Was it an accident?" Her voice said she knew the answer to that question even as she asked it. She turned to Amanda and swallowed hard. "The killer is waiting in the woods with a rifle right now, getting ready to shoot Lila." She furrowed her brow. "Calm down, Parker. It's not like being dead is the end of the world."

Amanda moved closer. "What's going on?"

"Lila's on her way over here from the Wagner place," Charley said. "Stanley gave her Parker's cell phone to plant in Carstairs' house like she planted the gun."

Amanda gave herself a mental slap upside the head. "In the kitchen drawer. That's where Jake said they found the gun. That's where Carstairs saw his blond wife's ghost, except it wasn't her ghost. It was Lila. Did Stanley give her the gun too? Did he kill you, Parker?"

"He says that's not important," Charley reported. Of course he did. "Mark says she's never going to make it here. The same guy who killed these men is going to shoot her as soon as she sets foot on Carstairs' property line. Parker's all weirded out. He wants us to save her."

"Save her from a man with a rifle? I vote no," Amanda said. "We'll call 911."

"Parker says there's no time. We've got to get to her before the shooter does."

"Parker, we're not a SWAT team," Amanda protested. "I didn't even bring a hand gun."

187

Teresa spun to face her. "You didn't? I thought you always packed."

"When I left home this morning, I was planning to visit Jake in the hospital. That's not something that requires artillery."

"But she's got a mouth on her," Charley said. "She could run them off with sarcastic snipes."

Amanda slid her cell phone from her pocket. "I'm calling 911."

Charley looked over her shoulder. "No, you're not. You don't have service."

Amanda returned her phone to her pocket. "Carstairs called 911 a lot. That means he has a land line. We've already entered a crime scene. I don't think a little breaking and entering will get us in much more trouble."

She strode up the weathered steps to the porch then stopped, her gaze caught by a dark, irregular stain that spread over a large section of the porch. A lump caught in her throat. The sad old man they'd talked to in jail had done this, spilled Jake's blood, almost killed him. It was hard to connect that event with the man who went in and out of reality, showing no signs of a cruel streak, but there was the evidence.

However, Jake would not have been on this porch if someone hadn't killed Parker. Her anger focused on the person who set this thing in motion, the one who killed Parker and the other men then callously dumped their bodies in the well.

If the latest ghost was to be believed, the Wagners had possession of Parker's cell phone and were using it to facilitate Lila's murder. If her body was found with his cell phone, she would be tied to his murder.

The Wagners were allied with the man waiting in the woods with a rifle. Was this how the other victims had died? Why? Lila used meth, the men in the well might have used meth. Was all this drug related? Was it that simple and that senseless?

The Wagner brothers practiced target shooting on Carstairs' property because they knew he never left the house. What else had they done on his property, knowing he'd never catch them doing it?

Cooked meth in partnership with the man with the rifle? Sold meth to Lila and the others? Killed them and tossed them in the well?

Again, why?

And where did Parker fit in?

The more they learned about this situation, the more questions she had.

Charley appeared on the porch, floating a couple of inches above one side of the stain. "I just checked. There's lots of guns and ammo in there, enough for an army. Guess the cops only took the murder weapon. There's enough for everybody to take a couple. Teresa, Parker, come on. We'll save Lila."

No one moved. No one spoke. An owl gave his eerie call from a tree close by, and a coyote howled in the distance. Amanda felt a tiny bit sorry for Charley.

"Oh." He dropped his head then lifted it and gave a lopsided grin. "Oops. Guess you and I won't be shooting anybody today, Parker, old man. It's up to us to do the planning and all the important stuff.

Come on, Amanda, let's go get guns for you and Teresa." He disappeared into the house again.

"Great idea, Charley," Teresa said, "except for the small detail that I've never shot in a gun in my life."

Amanda hesitated but only for an instant. She didn't like Lila, but she didn't want to see her killed. More importantly, she wanted to stop the two disgusting men who were responsible for the deaths of several people, including Parker, and she wanted to stay alive herself. "This is a good time to learn. I'll show you which end the bullet comes out. If nothing else, you can always pistol whip one of the jerks."

Amanda walked carefully around the blood stain to the front door. Of course it was locked, but the lock was old. She jiggled the knob a few times. She still wore her motorcycle gloves, so if they didn't get caught in the act, she wouldn't be leaving fingerprints. She laid her shoulder against the door and shoved.

It creaked then slid open.

The living room had probably once been comfortable and inviting, but Carstairs' wife and daughter had been dead a long time. A raggedy brown afghan covered most of the faded pattern on the beige sofa that might have started out in life as white. An empty coffee cup sat on a dusty table beside a recliner with a sagging seat. A black phone rested next to the coffee cup.

"In here!" Charley called.

Amanda lifted the receiver of the phone and was relieved to hear a dial tone. She punched in 911 and laid the receiver down. Someone would come to investigate. With any luck, they'd get there in time.

She followed the sound of Charley's voice to the master bedroom. A patchwork quilt lay half on and half off the king size bed. The rumpled sheets looked as if they hadn't been washed in a while. But the gun cabinet that covered almost an entire wall was dust free and filled with guns…shotguns like the one Carstairs had used to shoot Jake, rifles to hunt deer, and revolvers. No automatics and no polymer.

She slid open the glass doors, took out a Smith and Wesson .38, and checked the cylinder to be sure it was loaded.

"Omigawd!"

Amanda spun around at the sound, finger on the trigger.

Teresa threw her hands up and repeated, "Omigawd!"

"Sorry." Amanda lowered the gun. "I didn't hear you come in. I guess I was…" She indicated the weaponry.

"It freaked me out to see all those guns."

Amanda stuck the revolver in the waistband of her jeans. Not her favorite place to keep a weapon, but it would do for the moment. She lifted a Remington 870 pump shotgun from the rack, checked to be sure it was loaded, then extended it to Teresa. "This is the most devastating close-range gun around. Even if the guy's hopped up on meth, this will take him down."

Teresa licked her lips, cleared her throat and finally, tentatively, accepted the gun, holding it as if it were a piece of firewood oozing termites.

"Right hand here on the grip, left hand on the slide." She positioned Teresa's hands. "When you're ready to shoot—" she moved Teresa's right finger to the slide release button just in front of the trigger guard— "press this, pull the slide toward you and push it forward. That chambers a round. It may be all you have to do because just the sound of that can cause someone to have a heart attack. If the person doesn't keel over immediately, lift it to your shoulder, point in the general direction of your target, and squeeze the trigger. It will spray lead pellets over a wide area, pellets like the ones that hit Jake in the shoulder and took him down. You don't need to aim, just point."

Teresa lifted the gun to her shoulder then lowered it. "Press the button, pull this thing back, shove it forward, lift to my shoulder and fire."

"Pull, push and fire again until your target is on the ground or you run out of ammo."

Teresa swallowed. "And if I run out of ammo?"

"If you don't see his spirit leaving his body," Charley said, "grab the barrel and smack him with the stock."

Teresa grimaced. "Got it, I think. Okay, okay, Parker, we're coming!"

Amanda chose a Winchester 30-30 rifle for herself.

"Look at you," Charley said. "We've got our own personal SWAT team."

Amanda didn't quite share his enthusiasm. They'd come out to talk to a ghost or two, not to rescue Lila from some sniper hiding behind trees. She could only hope her 911 call brought the sheriff's department fast and, in the meantime, that Charley, Parker and the rest of the ghosts could help them steer clear of stray bullets.

Chapter Eighteen

The woods are lovely, dark, and deep.

The line from Robert Frost's poem flashed through Amanda's mind as they stepped off Carstairs' back porch. The woods before them were definitely dark and deep. Lovely wasn't a word she'd use to describe them, however. Scary, intimidating, creepy…but not lovely. Maybe if she hadn't known a killer was hiding somewhere in their depths.

A few yards from the back door a leafless tree reached skeletal arms toward the night sky. A breeze rustled the dead leaves still hanging onto a large oak. The usual chorus of night song was silent. That alone was enough to signal danger.

She descended the last step from the porch and Charley darted in front of her. "You forgot to close the door. I tried to close it, but I can't. You need to do it."

"I left the back door and the front door open for a reason. When the cops come to investigate the 911 call, they'll be able to figure out we went into the woods. Maybe they can find us." *In time to save us.*

"Don't worry," Charley said. "If they don't find us tonight, when everybody converges on the property tomorrow, they'll find us then."

194

Almost to the trees, Teresa halted and looked back. "Really, Charley? You think we're going to be here all night? Are you planning to get us killed so you'll have company?"

"No! I didn't mean it like that. I just…"

Amanda and Teresa waited.

"Come on, Parker, let's scout ahead then report back." Charley darted away, his faintly glowing form disappearing then reappearing as he progressed through and around the trees and underbrush.

Amanda touched the bulk of the revolver beneath her jacket to assure herself of its presence then tightened her grip on the rifle. "Well, I guess we should follow them."

"Yeah." Teresa swallowed so loudly Amanda could hear. "Parker says he can take us to Lila. Then all we have to do is be with her and she'll be safe."

Amanda scowled. "Really? That's all we have to do? Do you think he was such an annoying optimist in life?"

"I think he probably was. He also says he doesn't think the gunman will kill all of us."

"He doesn't *think* the man will kill *all* of us? I feel so much better now."

"He says that would be too many bodies to get rid of before the horde of lawmen descends tomorrow."

"That is so comforting." Amanda drew in a deep breath of the cool night air. Under other circumstances, she would describe it as clean, fresh, and invigorating. Tonight it was chilling. "All righty, then. We're off." She straightened her shoulders, lifted her chin and strode through the dry grass and leaves of the small clearing into the wooded area, each step taking her farther toward a woman who might be in danger and the man who was putting her in danger.

Though the land was flat and not heavily forested, there were enough trees that someone intent on murder wouldn't have a clear enough view to shoot from a hundred yards away. That would make him easier to spot. Much of the ground was covered with dead leaves and grass so it was unlikely someone could sneak up on them without being heard. On the other hand, anyone already waiting would hear them and be able to hide behind a tree. They could still venture past someone lurking in the shadows, prepared to blow them away.

Not exactly the way Amanda would have chosen to spend her evening.

She ducked under a low-hanging branch. A spider web grazed the side of her face. She shuddered and brushed it away. Yucky, but if it was the worst thing that happened tonight, she'd be thrilled.

She plunged through the woods. The sounds of her own heavy footsteps in her motorcycle boots and Teresa's lighter tread behind her made it impossible to hear anyone else. Or maybe her heart was pounding so loudly it drowned out all other sounds.

Charley's glowing form rushed up. "We found her!" He sounded breathless. Since he had no breath, was that possible? "Come on! Parker's with her." He beckoned them forward. "And try to walk a little quieter. You sound like a herd of buffalo."

"We don't have the benefit of being able to float above the ground," Amanda grumbled.

He made no comment but lowered himself so he appeared to be walking on his ankles. Soundlessly, of course.

They followed him to an old, barely visible trail. In the faint moonlight, Amanda would not have spotted it had he not pointed it out.

"Parker, we're on our way!" Charley yelled.

Amanda flinched even though she knew only she and Teresa could hear him. And Parker.

A shot exploded through the still autumn air and someone screamed.

Teresa shrieked and grabbed Amanda's arm.

"Your gun!" Amanda whispered. She lifted her own rifle and looked around, ready to fire.

"Press the button," Teresa mumbled, "pull this thing back—"

"Not yet!" All that stuff about not letting untrained people handle guns suddenly made a lot more sense. Maybe giving Teresa a loaded gun hadn't been such a good idea after all. "Just hang onto it and be ready. I'll let you know when."

Charley appeared in front of her, his faint glow pulsing. "Somebody's shooting at Lila!"

"Parker says the shooter's chasing her," Teresa reported.

Footsteps crunched loud and fast, coming toward them.

Lila or the killer or both?

Another shot, the sound crashing around them, closer this time, followed immediately by a brief, strangled scream.

The footsteps stopped.

Amanda held her breath.

Charley didn't move.

Teresa didn't speak.

The darkness deepened, wrapping the night tightly around them, threatening to smother them in its shadows.

Charley was the first to recover. "Come on!" He beckoned them forward.

Amanda ran. Not an easy task in her boots, but if she didn't maintain momentum, she might stand in place, frozen by fear.

Teresa panted behind her.

After this was over, maybe they should both take up aerobics, get in better shape.

If they survived this.

"She's hurt!" Charley called.

In the clearing just ahead Charley darted toward a prone figure. The woman's blond hair splayed around her head, dull in the darkness. At the edge of the clearing a man in camouflage lifted his rifle to his shoulder and aimed at her.

"Stop!" Amanda shouted. She raised her own rifle and fired over his head, into the trees.

The man looked at her and shifted the barrel of his gun in her direction.

She racked another shell into the chamber and aimed. No more warning shots.

The man cursed, turned and ran into the trees.

Damn. Wouldn't make for a good self defense plea if she shot him in the back.

"Lila!" Teresa squatted on the ground beside the woman. "Are you hurt?"

Lila groaned and lifted the hand that clutched her abdomen.

Gut shot. That was bad.

"Go get help, Teresa," Amanda instructed. "I'll stay with her."

"You go," Teresa said. "Parker wants to talk to her through me."

"There's a man out there with a big gun, and if he comes back, what if you get confused and push before you pull? Parker can talk to her later." Though when she looked at the amount of blood on the ground beside Lila, Amanda wasn't sure there would be a *later* for her.

"I can talk to Parker!" Charley settled on the other side of Lila. "Uhh, she's bleeding a lot."

"That looks bad," Teresa said.

"Go! The sheriff's people may already be at Carstairs' house. If they're not, hang up the phone and call for an ambulance. Hurry! Leave the gun and run as fast as you can."

Teresa stood. "I can't run very fast."

"Then walk fast. Crawl fast. I don't care, just get help."

Teresa crunched away into the darkness.

Amanda knelt beside Lila.

"It hurts." She coughed.

Amanda pulled off her motorcycle jacket and placed it on the wound, holding it as tightly as she could in an effort to stop the flow of blood. "Hang on. Help is on the way."

"It's my fault," Lila whispered.

"That you got shot? I don't think so."

"I didn't know he was a senator's son. I thought he was just another homeless meth head, a man nobody would miss, like the others."

"Are you talking about Steven Anderson?"

"Parker wants to talk to her," Charley said.

"I don't really care," Amanda snapped. "Parker, I've had it with you. You had plenty of time to talk before this. If you'd told us who killed you, this might not have happened. Lila, what about Steven Anderson?"

Lila rolled her head from side to side. "Stanley was mad, so mad. He put Parker in the well for me and then the cops found him and the senator's son and now it's a big deal and his client paid him for one more hunt. I didn't want to bring him another man but he said I owed him. It's not good to owe Stanley."

"What? Stanley put Parker in the well? Another hunt? What are you talking about?"

"Parker gave me money so I didn't have to work for Stanley, but then…" She blinked a couple of times and tried to sit up. "Parker?"

A chill darted down Amanda's spine. Was Lila calling to Parker's memory for comfort or could she see him? If she could see him, did that mean…?

Amanda gently pushed her back down. "Lie still until the paramedics get here. Did Stanley kill Parker?"

The tears flowed freely down Lila's face. "Parker, I didn't mean to shoot you."

Amanda drew in a deep breath. That answered her question.

"He says he knows it was an accident," Charley said quietly.

"My whole life was awful until you came along. I really believed you were my brother and I loved you so much. You were the best family I ever had. When you said I wasn't really your sister, I didn't want to live."

Was Lila babbling nonsense or revealing secrets? "You aren't really his sister?"

Lila lifted a hand to her forehead and groaned.

"What's she talking about, Parker?" Charley asked. He listened for a moment. "Ross is such a forensics geek, he'd never have accepted her without a DNA test, so Parker had one done and found out they're not related." His voice was unusually soft. Amanda would have called it *sympathetic* if she'd thought Charley was capable of that emotion. "When he told her, she ran in the bedroom, grabbed the gun and pointed it at her head."

"You tried to stop me, and I don't know anything about guns. I'm sorry. It just went off. So much blood. I had to put Mama's rug down to hide the blood. Every time I see it, I remember." She began to sob.

The rug in her bedroom. She'd sunk down onto it, not because she was dizzy from drugs but because she was grieving for what she'd done.

"He's comforting her." Charley looked at a point in space beside Lila.

Lila drew a shaky hand over her eyes, making an ineffectual attempt to wipe away her tears. "I'm so glad you're not mad at me."

Amanda was pretty sure it wasn't a good sign that Lila could see Parker.

Lila's features suddenly relaxed as if the pain had abated. The corners of her mouth twisted slightly upward. "You talked to my mother? Did you ask her why she put your daddy's name on my birth certificate if he wasn't my daddy?"

The eerie silence again settled around them with Lila's ragged breathing the only sound.

"His dad was nice to her mother," Charley said, "took care of her, drove her to the hospital to have her baby. She didn't want Lila's real father to have any rights to her because he was a drunk, had abused her, and left when he found out she was pregnant. When the doctor asked for the father's name, she gave the name of the one man who'd been kind to her."

Lila's eyes welled with tears again. "My real daddy didn't want me?"

Charley's glow brightened. "Parker says her real father was an idiot, that he missed out on a great daughter."

Lila's pain-filled gaze turned toward Charley. "Who are you?"

Oh, damn. Now she could see Charley too. That didn't bode well at all.

"I'm with her." Charley pointed to Amanda.

Lila bit her lip and looked away from Charley, back to the empty space next to him. "I want to be your family, Parker. I want to be your sister." She lifted her hand into the air and gave a weak smile. Her gaze softened and became unfocused. "I want to be with you."

Amanda pushed her hand to the ground. "Don't even think about it. You're staying right here until Teresa gets back with somebody to help you."

"Amanda," Charley said, "I think—"

"Shut up, Charley. Lila, look at me. Stop looking at Parker. Look at me." She waved her free hand in front of Lila's face. "Over here! Land of the living. Stay here. Want a cigarette? I'll get you a cigarette if you'll stay here and smoke it."

Lila blinked and for an instant her eyes focused on Amanda. "A cigarette?" she whispered. "I'm trying to quit. Parker helped me quit smoking and using meth, but then I shot him and had to ask Stanley to help me get rid of the body and I was weak, so weak. I went back to cigarettes and drugs. I was only strong when you were here to help me." Soft light radiated from her body.

Amanda scowled at Charley. "Are you doing that?"

He shook his head. "No."

Lila raised her hand again and clutched invisible fingers.

Amanda reached to push her arm down, but there was no need. It dropped to the earth of its own accord. The luminescence faded and her eyes dimmed.

"Lila, get back here!" Amanda continued to hold her jacket over the wound though she knew there was no longer any reason to do so.

"They're leaving!" Charley said. "Parker, don't go! Come back. What about me? I'm your friend! No, I don't see any white light! Just because it's there doesn't mean you have to run into it! Don't leave me!"

Another shot exploded and a heavy weight crashed into Amanda's left shoulder, knocking her backward. An instant later pain screamed through her arm.

Damnation! She'd been shot!

Chapter Nineteen

"Run!" Charley shouted.

Amanda would have to get up before she could run and she didn't think standing would be a good idea with a shooter out there. However she was in agreement with the general idea of Charley's advice. She needed to get away.

She rolled, turning briefly onto the injured arm, stifling the urge to scream.

Another shot hit the ground behind her, exactly where she was lying an instant before.

She rolled faster, against a tree trunk, twisted around it, reaching the other side just as a bullet hit the tree.

Someone was serious about killing her.

She slid the revolver from her waistband, got to her feet, and fired in the direction the shot had come from.

Charley darted over to her. "I'm sorry! I was watching Parker and Lila and you almost got killed because I wasn't guarding you."

"Save it for later. Where is he?"

"There's three of them now."

Three of them, one of her, and four rounds left in her revolver. Both Teresa's shotgun and her rifle lay in the middle of the clearing. Even if she could get to one of them, she wasn't sure she could lift and aim it with the damaged shoulder.

Someone moved stealthily through the underbrush in the area across the clearing. She could hear the rustling, but no more shots came, no flash she could aim at.

"Go stand in front of one of them and I'll shoot through you," she whispered.

Charley clutched his stomach. "That could hurt."

"Then move out of the way as soon as you see the bullet heading toward you." It was a ridiculous statement, but no more ridiculous than the idea a bullet could hurt him. "You fell down on your job as lookout. This is the least you can do."

Charley crossed the clearing, into the woods. Amanda lifted her gun and gazed down the sight, following his darting movements. Why did he keep moving? Was he having trouble finding her attackers?

"I'm glad you're here!" Charley shouted.

Who was he talking to? Had Teresa returned with help?

He dashed back across the clearing. "The boys from the well are here. Mark said the Wagner brothers and the hunter are circling around, trying to get behind you. Duck!"

She turned to look just as the woods exploded with sound again and a bullet seared past her face, into the tree beside her.

Amanda dropped to her knees, her gaze searching the area.

"Thanks, Grant!" Charley moved a few feet and stopped, waving. "Over here, Amanda!"

Amanda aimed at his chest and squeezed the trigger. A man screamed.

"Good shot!" Charley reported. "He's down!"

Amanda made a mental note to forgive Charley for his next five offenses.

"Thanks, Winston! Over here, Amanda! Quick! He's aiming at you!"

Amanda spun, aimed at Charley's glowing chest, and fired. Another scream followed by a wild shot that went over her head.

Make that his next ten offenses.

One shooter and two bullets left. Her odds were improving…assuming Charley had been standing directly in front of the guys she'd just shot and they were completely incapacitated.

Charley darted back and forth through the trees. "We're looking! Get down!"

So much for her odds improving. Time for some trash talk.

"There's only one of you left out there," she shouted. "I can see you. The ghosts of the men you put down that well are helping me. They want me to kill all of you. I'm giving you the chance to take your buddies back home before they bleed out."

No response except the sound of someone moving on her left.

"Stanley's aiming at you around the tree! Get his arm! Right here!" Charley held his hand out.

Damn. Tough shot.

She took it.

Stanley cursed.

"Got him!" Charley pumped a triumphant fist into the air.

But it was only Stanley's arm and rustlings from behind her and to the right told her the other men were still alive.

She ran to where Charley stood. "Don't move, Stanley," she ordered, pleased that her voice sounded strong, wasn't shaking the way her insides were.

Stanley gaped at her and reached for his rifle with his uninjured hand.

Amanda shot that arm and put a booted foot on the rifle. "I said, don't move!" She held her empty revolver close to his face. "Unless your buddies want me to blow your ugly face to the other side of your head, they better stop moving too." She could only hope nobody had been counting shots.

Stanley stood motionless, blood dripping from his right hand and his left elbow. She held her own injured shoulder to the side, hoping he wouldn't see her wound. He was a big man and even with his injuries, he might be able to take her if she didn't get her bluff in and keep it until Teresa returned with help.

"Clyde and another guy are up and coming this way," Charley reported. "They've both got rifles, but they're hurt. Get them all over here. You can control them better if they're in the same place."

Charley's knowledge of criminal activities did come in handy from time to time.

She cocked the hammer on the empty gun and pointed it at his nose. "Your murder victims tell me your buddies are headed this way. You better tell them to drop their weapons and get over here or I'm going to shoot them again as soon as I finish with you."

"Bitch has got a gun in my face!" Stanley shouted. "She's crazy! Drop your guns and come here!"

"The ghosts will tell me if you all don't do as he says," Amanda threatened.

"I don't know if I can!" The voice was wheezy. "I'm hurt bad. I need help."

"Mark says the hunter's lifting his rifle."

"Put that gun down!" Amanda shouted. "Didn't I warn you? You're starting to make me mad, and when I get mad, people die. Get your sorry butts over here. Now!"

"Who are you?" Stanley sounded anxious and unsure. Good.

"I'm your worst nightmare." She tried to look scary instead of scared.

Clyde staggered up beside his brother. He held one hand to his chest and wheezed. Bullet probably hit a lung. He could be in trouble if help didn't arrive soon.

He'd tried to kill her. She didn't care if help didn't arrive soon.

The third man, a stranger, sidled up to join them. He clutched his side with one hand. Though blood flowed through his fingers, he seemed to be in better shape than the others and still held his rifle in his other hand.

"Put it down," she ordered.

"No."

"If you don't set that gun on the ground, I'm going to blow your friend's head off."

The man sneered. "You think I care what you do to him?"

She stepped back and aimed at the man. "Then I'll put a hole in your right side to match the one in your left, but before I do, the men you killed want to torture you, pay you back for what you did to them. They're going to make the bullet hole you already have hurt really bad." She looked at Charley and tilted her head toward the stranger. "They're going to make it cold as ice and hurt really, really bad."

Charley stared at the man, his expression blank.

The man lifted his rifle and sneered. "Is that right? *Really, really bad*?"

"Like a *Charley* horse in your gut."

"Oh! You want me to…I got it!" Charley ran toward the man and punched him in his bullet wound.

The man grunted and slumped forward.

"Drop the gun or I'll do it again," Charley warned.

Of course he hadn't heard Charley, but he slowly opened his fingers and let the rifle fall to the ground.

Now if she could just continue to hold them at bay until help arrived.

"Do you know who you're dealing with?" the hunter asked. He didn't have the country accent of the brothers, he was better groomed, and his clothing looked expensive.

Amanda lifted her chin and gave him her best condescending glare. "Of course I know who you are." She didn't.

"His name is Blake Morrissey," Charley said. "He used to pay the Wagners to hunt deer, but now he pays them to let him hunt men."

Amanda sucked in a sharp breath. She'd known this involved murder…but hunting human beings like deer? She fixed her gaze on the shooter. "Blake Morrissey."

His eyes widened. His smug self-confidence slipped a notch.

"You killed these men. You were bored with hunting deer and wanted a more challenging prey."

"Help me!" a new voice called.

Charley turned toward the sound. "It's the man from the alley, the one Lila had in the back seat of her car."

I didn't want to bring him this one…

Lila had brought this man to Stanley?

"Over here!" Amanda shouted. "Looks like we have a new guest at our little party." Three murderers, one druggie, Charley, and four victims from the well. The woods were was getting downright crowded.

The skinny, bearded man from the alley staggered toward them. A ragged tear ripped one side of his dirty T-shirt and scratches covered his face. "Help me." He moved closer to Stanley who flinched backward. "Just give me a little more. I swear it's the last time." The man scratched his arms and tugged at his shirt, tearing it more. "I got money. I can pay. Just one hit."

Was he begging Stanley for meth?

Amanda recalled Carstairs' stories of strange people around his house, a naked man at his door, asking for help, scratching himself until he bled.

And Lila's words.

I thought he was just another homeless meth head, a man nobody would miss, like the others.

The skinny man took a step in her direction, but Charley pushed through him. He shivered and looked at her accusingly. "I'm cold. That hurt."

"Keep away from her or I'll hurt you worse," Charley warned.

Amanda took a step backward, putting space between her and all of them. "You paid Lila to bring you men off the street so this monster—" she nodded toward Morrissey— "could hunt them down and kill them like animals. You thought they were homeless drug addicts nobody would miss but you were wrong."

"I ain't no drug addict." The skinny man backed away.

Stanley's eyes narrowed to glowing slits of hate. "I wasn't wrong. They were just meth heads that nobody cared about. Everything was fine until that stupid slut killed her own brother and called me, crying and begging me to help her. She didn't tell me his brother was a cop, and she was too dumb to know the one she brought before him was a senator's son. Suddenly the whole state of Texas is coming after us.

This is all her fault. Bitch couldn't do anything right."

Amanda slapped him in the jaw with her .38. "They're all people. They have names and families who miss them." She looked over Stanley's head. "Can you hear them? The men you killed? They're here, and they're talking about you. They want the world to know what you did to them. They want to see you arrested and punished."

The skinny man looked all around him. "I hear them!"

Stanley wiped blood from his mouth and sneered. "You start telling people about ghosts talking to you and they're going to lock you up, not me. Lila's dead with her brother's cell phone in her pocket. She's not talking. You're the crazy woman who talks to ghosts and shot the three of us while we were trying to save Lila."

"You can't hear the ghosts of your victims?" Amanda asked. "Tell me about what he did to you all."

"Stanley held them prisoner until they were jonesing for drugs," Charley reported, "then he gave them fifteen minutes head start before Blake went after them."

Amanda repeated the information. "Hit them again, guys, all of them." She looked at Charley.

He zipped past the three of them, punching them in their wounds as he went.

Stanley's eyes widened but he said nothing. Blake flinched and also remained silent.

Clyde moaned and sank to his knees. Poor monster might not make it. "We had to do something. The government was going to steal our land. We couldn't pay the taxes. Our family's lived here for five generations. This land is ours! We had to save it! It was his idea."

Amanda wasn't sure if he was accusing Blake Morrissey or his brother, but Stanley responded.

"Shut up, you idiot."

Amanda looked at Morrissey. "Big hunter. Able to track down men out of their minds from drug withdrawal. Are you proud of yourself?"

The man's eyes blazed with anger. Maybe she'd pushed it a little too far. His gaze never leaving hers, he stooped and wrapped his hand around the stock of his rifle then stood.

"Put that down!"

"I don't think so." He withdrew his hand from his bloody side and lifted the rifle to his shoulder.

"Run!" Charley shouted.

"Really? That's the best you've got? Run? Hit him again!"

Charley punched Blake Morrissey's bleeding wound again.

He flinched but didn't waver. His finger moved to the trigger.

He'd called her bluff.

"Shoot the bitch," Stanley encouraged.

"Help me!" The skinny man rushed toward her.

Amanda turned and ran, darting around a tree, searching for cover.

Behind her Blake Morrissey laughed. "Another hunt with a more worthy adversary."

"This way," Charley directed.

She followed his glow, unsure which direction they were headed.

"Over here." He was beckoning to someone she couldn't see. Another ghost?

A shot burst through the night from somewhere behind her.

The sounds of people running through dead leaves and dry grass came from all directions.

Amanda ran blindly toward Charley, tripped over something in the dark and felt herself falling. No, no, no, no!

Arms came out of the darkness, grabbed her, pulled her against a solid body. Anger, fear, and a red fury exploded through her. She twisted, jabbed her elbow into the body, kicked backward, satisfied when her boot connected with something and her attacker cursed.

"Amanda! Stop!"

She wasn't about to stop. These men were evil, killed without mercy.

She lifted her foot to kick again, then the voice registered. "Teresa?"

"It's me! That man you're trying to kill is Sheriff Laskey."

She dropped her foot and Laskey released his hold on her.

"They're out there! Stanley and his brother and a horrible man named Morrissey and a drug addict."

She waved her arms but was so turned around she wasn't sure where they were.

Laskey and two deputies looked in various directions. "Where?" Laskey asked.

"Follow me!" Charley plunged through the trees. "My friends are taking care of them."

The sheriff's men couldn't see Charley, but she could. "This way." She started after him.

Teresa put a hand on her arm. "You're hurt."

Sudden pain shot through her arm and shoulder. Amanda gave a shaky laugh. "I guess I am. I forgot. Adrenalin."

"Stay here. I'll handle this. Come on, guys. I love it when men follow me." Teresa headed after Charley.

Laskey nodded, and the deputies went with Teresa while he stayed behind. "We've got paramedics on the way." Laskey looked at her arm. "Ms. Landow said somebody was hurt really bad. This doesn't look too bad."

"Someone else. She didn't make it." Amanda shivered. "She's around here somewhere close, in a clearing. Her name's Lila Stone." No more nameless victims.

"We'll find her."

"Sheriff's department!" someone shouted. "Put it down! You're under arrest!"

What beautiful words!

"We need a paramedic over here," the same voice shouted. "Three men shot, one's in bad shape, and one guy's having big-time drug withdrawal."

Laskey looked at Amanda.

"I did it. I shot them all. Self defense. It's a long story."

"We'll get you to the hospital and take your statement later."

Teresa and Charley returned to Amanda's side.

"Got 'em," Charley said. "The men were really happy. They thanked me and then they left. Guess they went into that stupid light too."

Laskey looked at Teresa. "Can you take care of her? Get her to a doctor? We need to deal with these men and find the woman who was killed."

"Lila Stone," Amanda repeated. "Her name is Lila Stone."

"I'll get Amanda to the hospital," Teresa said.

"We'll finish up here and meet you there." Laskey headed in the direction his deputies had gone.

"You okay to walk back to the car?" Teresa asked.

"Of course." Amanda felt exhausted and exhilarated at the same time.

"Charley said Parker left with Lila."

"Yeah." As they walked through the woods back to Carstairs' house, she told Teresa the entire story.

At the end of the journey, the three of them settled into Teresa's car for the ride to the hospital.

"I miss Parker," Charley said. "And it was fun talking to those other guys tonight. But they all left me."

"Maybe you could go with them," Amanda suggested. "Into the light. It must be a good thing. They seemed eager to do it, right?"

Charley clenched his lips and looked through the windshield into the night. "I don't see any light. I'm not going anywhere."

The exhilaration fled leaving Amanda with only exhaustion.

Chapter Twenty

Kraken County Hospital was small. Clyde and Blake were admitted and stowed away in rooms to be treated. The drug addict scheduled to be Blake's next victim was taken to the sheriff's department to give his statement, would probably spend the night in a warm jail cell, then be taken to a shelter or a rehab center. Amanda hoped the night's experience would point him in a different direction.

Since her injury was deemed minor, Amanda was taken to the emergency room…and so was Stanley. With two bullet holes and broken bones in his hand and arm, the only doctor on duty judged him to need treatment before Amanda who had suffered only a flesh wound. She waited on a hard examination table while Charley drifted around beside her. Had it been a soft bed, had he not been there, had her arm not hurt so badly, she would have gone to sleep. She had never been so tired in all her life.

Teresa pulled back the curtain, entered, and handed Amanda her cell phone. "Okay, I called your sister. You owe me."

Amanda took the phone. "Thanks. I just wasn't up to talking to her—"

"You mean listening to her," Charley said.

Teresa nodded. "She was pretty excited. Dinner's ruined, and I think she's planning your funeral."

"You told her I'm okay, right?" Amanda asked.

"I didn't really get past the part about you being shot and brought here."

"Oh, well. I'll be home before she gets the funeral invitations sent out. Having them engraved will take a while."

Someone cursed from the other side of the flimsy partition that separated her from Stanley.

Amanda slid off the table.

"What are you doing?" Teresa asked.

Amanda pushed aside the curtain and leaned around the partition. Stanley sat on a table that matched hers. One sleeve of his red plaid shirt had been cut off at the elbow, the other at the shoulder. A doctor pressed the contents of a syringe into his arm. His face was pale, his lips clenched. He looked to be in a great deal of pain. "Stitch him up with no anesthetic, doc."

The sheriff's deputy standing in the corner stepped forward. "Ma'am, you shouldn't be in here."

"I know, but I really want to see him suffer some more."

Stanley glared. "Bitch."

"Ma'am—"

Teresa grabbed the back of her T-shirt and tugged.

"Okay, okay." She returned to her cubicle and slid onto the table. "I feel better knowing that worthless piece of scum is suffering."

The curtain parted. Ross stood behind a wheelchair. Jake sat in that wheelchair.

Teresa ran to Ross and he pulled her into his arms, holding her tightly.

Amanda slid off the table and Charley darted between her and Jake. "What's he doing here?"

Jake rose shakily. One arm was in a sling, but he was free of tubes and appeared more sober than he'd been that morning.

"What are you doing here?" Amanda looked down, expecting to see his bare legs. He'd managed to get his jeans on. Darn.

Jake sank onto the table beside her. Beads of sweat dotted his pale face and he was breathing hard.

"I called him," Ross said. He still had one arm wrapped tightly around Teresa. "I've been monitoring alerts from Laskey's office because my brother's body was found in his jurisdiction. Imagine my surprise when I saw that Teresa Landow was requesting assistance for Lila Stone."

"She's dead," Teresa said. "We tried to help her but we couldn't."

"She killed your brother," Amanda said. Ross stiffened. "But it was an accident. She was trying to kill herself."

"Did my brother tell you this?"

"No, Lila did."

"Parker had a DNA test done to verify that she was his sister," Teresa said. "She wasn't, and it broke her heart."

Ross shook his head slowly. "She wasn't his sister? What about the birth certificate?"

"I'll explain it all later. They were very close. Your brother cared for her like a sister. He couldn't justify letting her have money that was rightly yours, but he was still worried about her. He left with her spirit when she died."

"My brother's spirit is gone?" Ross asked.

"Yes. He went into the light." Even from across the cubicle, Amanda could feel Teresa's tension as she waited for Ross' response.

The curtain opened again and Sheriff Laskey came in, diverting everyone's attention. He looked surprised to see Ross and Jake. "Evening, officers."

"Evening, Sheriff."

He shifted his gun belt uncomfortably as he looked first at Teresa then Amanda. "So, Morrissey and the Wagner brothers think you both see ghosts."

Teresa lifted her chin. "I am a medium, yes. I have spoken with the victims from the well, and I can give you names if you'd like to verify them."

Teresa told her story about Parker and the men from the well leading them to Lila, but she didn't mention Charley. She was giving Amanda the chance to continue to keep her secret.

Amanda studied Ross for his reaction. His expression remained the same as Teresa talked.

Then it was time for Amanda to tell her story of what happened after Teresa went for help.

"Morrissey and the Wagners started shooting at me," she said. "I shot back."

Everyone in the room waited.

"I'm a better shot than they are."

"I stood in front of the men so you could aim at them!" Charley exclaimed. "Do I get any credit?"

"You told them the ghosts of the men they killed were there," Laskey said.

This was it. Her chance to admit to seeing Charley, admit that he'd helped her. "Yes, I did tell them the ghosts of their victims were there." It was true as far as it went. She just needed to finish the story, confess about Charley.

Laskey narrowed his eyes.

Amanda licked her lips. Teresa was brave enough to tell the truth and risk ridicule. She had to do the same.

The doctor slid the curtain aside. "Miss Caulfield, I'm Doctor Osborne."

"Well," Laskey said, "if you'll both agree to come in tomorrow and give your official statements, I'll go home and get some sleep."

"Okay." Amanda wasn't sure if she was relieved or upset that her moment of truth had been interrupted. Probably relieved.

"We'll be there," Teresa promised.

Laskey left.

Teresa took Ross' arm with one hand and Charley's with the other. "Let's go down the hall. I can't stand the sight of blood."

"No!" Charley protested. "I don't want to go with you!"

He had no choice. He followed her out.

Ross drew the curtain behind them, but his soft words came through clearly. "I'd still love you even if you told me you talk to little green men from Mars."

"I'm going to puke!" Charley shouted. "Right here in the hospital, I'm going to puke!"

Amanda looked at Jake. He was smiling. Even the doctor was smiling. Ross accepted Teresa with all her quirks. Surely Jake would do the same for her. She was going to tell him about Charley.

But not right now. Too many people around.

Ross and Teresa's footsteps disappeared down the hall.

Jake slid from the table onto the chair beside it. "You think she'll live, doc?"

The doctor examined Amanda's wound. "A couple of stitches and she'll be good as new."

Amanda endured the process with gritted teeth. She wasn't going to wimp out in front of Jake.

The doctor finished and put on a clean bandage. "You're good to go. I can write you a prescription for pain pills if you'd like."

Amanda shook her head. "I'll be fine." And if she wasn't, a glass or two of wine should help.

The doctor left the cubicle.

She was alone with Jake. Time to confess.

"So in one evening you shot three men and beat up the sheriff?" Jake's eyes glowed as he looked at her.

"I didn't know it was the sheriff."

"I'm going to have to keep closer tabs on you, protect the citizens of Texas from you." He reached for her hand.

She wrapped her fingers around his. "I like that plan."

She slid off the table, and Jake rose shakily from his chair. He leaned over and touched his lips to hers.

The events of the evening faded. The pain in her arm disappeared. All she felt was the magic of Jake's kiss.

The curtain rings screamed as someone shoved the curtain aside.

"Amanda!" Her very pregnant sister waddled into the room.

Sunny followed close behind.

Jake released her and stepped back.

"We were so worried about you!" Jenny tried to hug her.

Amanda flinched. "Ouch. Bullet wound."

Jenny lifted her hand to her mouth. "I'm sorry! I invited your friend for dinner. I wanted to surprise you, but then you didn't come home and dinner got cold, and we were afraid something had happened to you, and it had!"

"Sunny was the surprise? You didn't redo the living room?"

"I decided to name the baby Suzanne Amanda. I just have a feeling she's going to have red hair so I want to name her after my sister and my sister's friend who both have red hair."

Amanda and Sunny exchanged surprised glances.

It was always possible Jenny's baby would have red hair, but it would have to come from Davey's genes.

Jenny's eyes suddenly widened and she clutched her stomach. "Oh, I'm having more of those brackish contractions! Ow! That hurts!"

If Amanda had a bullet wound, her sister had to have worse pain.

Jenny winced. "I think I need to sit down."

"Uh, Jenny," Sunny said, looking at the floor, "I think your water broke. I believe you are going to have that baby right now."

Amanda took her sister's arm. "Thank goodness we're in a hospital."

Panic spread over Jake's face. "I'll go find a doctor." He rushed past his wheelchair and out of the cubicle.

"I can't have the baby here!" Jenny protested.

"I'm not sure you have a choice." Sunny took her other arm and steered her toward the chair beside the exam table.

"No! I need my doctor and my hospital and…and where's Davey? I can't have this baby without my Davey!"

Where's Davey?

My Davey?

Jenny scrambled in her purse and produced her cell phone.

Jenny was calling Davey. She was having the baby and all was well with her and Davey.

That meant Amanda would have her apartment back. She would even be happy to sleep on the lavender sheets. Who could see color in the dark?

Doctor Osborne rushed back into the cubicle.

"I can't have this baby here! This isn't my hospital! I'm calling my husband! He'll take me to my hospital in Dallas! Don't let me have this baby here all alone!"

"Relax, ma'am," the doctor soothed. "We can move you to another hospital. If your water just broke and this is your first baby, I'm sure you'll have plenty of time. Let me get you a gown and do an exam."

"We'll give you some privacy," Amanda said.

"Yes," Sunny agreed. "We'll go find a Coke."

They hurried through the curtain before Jenny could protest, though Amanda wasn't sure she would have. She was talking to Davey.

Jake leaned against the wall.

"Jake, nice to see you again," Sunny said.

"Do you know where there's a Coke machine?" Amanda asked.

"Down the hall. I'll show you," Jake said.

Sunny looked from one to the other of them. "I think I'll pass on the Coke. You seem to be okay, and I can't do anything to help your sister. I'm going to head home."

Amanda gave her a one-armed hug. "Thank you for worrying about me. I'm sorry the evening turned out so badly."

"I got to see you. It was worth it. Good night, Jake."

Amanda watched her birth mother walk down the hall. How lucky she was to have Sunny in her life. Much as she hated to admit it, she had to thank Charley for the bizarre circumstances that led her to Sunny.

"I like her," Jake said. "No wonder you're friends. She reminds me a lot of you."

Another secret she needed to share with Jake if they were going to have a relationship. "Let's find that Coke machine, get you back to your room, and have another kiss."

"Good idea." He wrapped his unbandaged arm around her unbandaged shoulder and pulled her to him. "But not necessarily in that order."

One of these days she'd share her secrets, but not tonight.

THE END

About the Author:

I grew up in a small rural town in southeastern Oklahoma where our favorite entertainment on summer evenings was to sit outside under the stars and tell stories. When I went to bed at night, instead of a lullaby, I got a story. That could be due to the fact that everybody in my family has a singing voice like a bullfrog with laryngitis, but they sure could tell stories—ghost stories, funny stories, happy stories, scary stories.

For as long as I can remember I've been a storyteller. Thank goodness for computers so I can write down my stories. It's hard to make listeners sit still for the length of a book! Like my family's tales, my stories are funny, scary, dramatic, romantic, paranormal, magic.

Besides writing, my interests are reading, eating chocolate and riding my Harley.

Contact information is available on my website. I love to talk to readers! And writers. And riders. And computer programmers. Okay, I just plain love to talk!

http://www.sallyberneathy.com

Manufactured by Amazon.ca
Bolton, ON

33526210R00129